DEATH DISCOVERS A BONE

THE PENELOPE STANDING MYSTERIES
BOOK 6

TESS BAYTREE

Cover image created using the following assets licensed from DepositPhotos: 249601500, 330843764, 18915111, 751767028, 37715963, 134208664

ONE

According to Benjamin Franklin, nothing was certain aside from death and taxes. Penelope added a third item to the list as she trotted up the steep slope of the historic cemetery: fences falling over in anything stronger than a light breeze. At least, that held true for the fences built by Red and Sons, which included nearly all the backyards in town.

Still, the hunt for a missing dog was a good excuse to spend time walking through the old cemetery. In the newer cemetery outside the city limits, where most current burials were done, the ground was covered with a perfect carpet of grass, easy to maintain and mow since the pre-approved markers with their identical fonts and curated messages were flush with the ground. Penelope preferred the more comfortable mess of the old cemetery, with its irregular stone markers tipping drunkenly as time and tree roots pushed them aside.

Maybe in another ten or twenty years, Penelope would appreciate the flat smooth paths of the new cemetery, but though she'd more or less accepted she was middle-aged —

fifties were middle-aged in her mind — she was still active enough to enjoy the beauty of a more natural state.

Ahead, a flash of tan fur confirmed that Esther's tip had been valid. Sightings of Zoomy had come in from multiple people that morning. Either the mischievous dog had run around half the town or there was a second yellow lab roaming the area. Penelope pretended to look at the inscription on the headstone in front of her, shook the bag of dog treats, and waited until she saw Zoomy peek out from behind a mausoleum. "Gotcha!" she whispered. The trick now was to convince Zoomy to come over for attention instead of running away again.

The glint of a metal shovel reflecting the sun caught Penelope's attention. Close to the rosebushes surrounding the cemetery perimeter, a man in a gray suit talked to a man in mud-stained clothing and heavy boots as they both walked away from a huge mound of dirt. A beautiful rosebush was in full bloom on the other side of an open grave. Both of the men looked vaguely familiar; place association allowed Penelope to recognize them as Derek Smith, the head of the town's cemetery committee, and Matteo Faulkner, the caretaker, who always seemed to have a layer of mud on the back of his shirt. Both men had very strong opinions about dogs — especially dogs not on a leash — in the cemetery.

Not wanting to listen to yet another lecture on the subject, Penelope eased behind a cement statue. Given the wings, she assumed it was meant to be an angel, but when set against the classically beautiful statue of Rafael three rows over, this unfortunate lump of cement was like a pug compared to a wolf. The eyes even bulged in the same way.

From the safety of the inbred seraphim, Penelope

scanned the cemetery for something to excuse her presence so Derek wouldn't automatically blame her for the loose dog. Esther had to be around here somewhere, since she was acting as a representative of the Rose Garden Society to make sure some special rosebush wasn't damaged by the digging. Penelope could claim she was there to visit.

There! On the gravel path next to the fresh dirt pile, partially hidden by the huge rosebush with pink and yellow flowers, her friend Esther sat in her wheelchair. Penelope crinkled the treat bag and pointedly ignored the dog as she angled her steps toward Esther.

Esther's gray curls were windblown, and there were ruts in the gravel where her wheelchair's tires had lost traction, but she looked as unbothered as always. After a long career teaching kindergarten, not much rattled Esther. She looked up from her phone when Penelope hiked across the grass. "How goes the hunt?"

"You were right. That's Zoomy." Penelope had been looking for the dog between other pet sitting appointments for the last three days. "Did they find enough of Elmer to put into the box? Or are they just going to throw in some dirt and call it a day?"

Esther shook her head. "No. It's not Elmer. Matteo found a metal plaque for Josephine Harper." She pointed halfway down the hill. "Josephine is supposed to be there."

"Ah."

Unlike Zoomy, Elmer was human, or had been before his demise thirty years before. After seven decades of carefully avoiding all danger, Elmer had thrown caution to the winds and booked a skydiving trip for his birthday. While walking across the tarmac, he'd sneezed, inhaled his dental bridge, and choked before anyone had noticed he hadn't climbed into the plane. After such a noteworthy death, his burial had been unremarkable — apparently in more ways than one.

Penelope leaned over to look into the hole. The local soil had more clay than dirt, which could make digging like trying to cut through cement, but Matteo had prepared by soaking the ground overnight. The sides of the hole were professionally squared off, done by hand since the hill was too steep and uneven to use mechanical equipment. At the bottom, the mud had been wiped from a metal plaque attached to a remarkably flat surface, though Penelope couldn't read the writing. She'd assumed anything left buried more than a few years would be in even worse shape than the Red & Sons fence responsible for Zoomy's current freedom. "How long ago was Josephine buried? That coffin's in amazingly good shape."

"Forty years, give or take," Esther said. "The casket is stainless steel. She spent half her savings on it when she got sick. Her brother tried to bully her out of it, so she changed her will and left the rest to a cat sanctuary."

That brought a smile to Penelope's face, because that sort of spiteful response was exactly what she would have done. Josephine might have been a good friend if they'd known each other. "So if Josephine is here..." She stopped staring down at the stainless steel casket, and looked up the hill. Matteo and Derek had unrolled a thick stack of A-sized paper against the Stanhope mausoleum and were pointing at headstones and then flipping through the stack. It looked like they'd brought along every version of the cemetery map produced since the town had been founded.

Esther shook her head. "It might not mean anything. For a couple decades, Massimo Faulkner — Matteo's great-uncle — and Thea Harding — she was in charge of the cemetery committee at the time — refused to speak to each other. Sometimes Massimo dug graves in a more convenient place, and when the headstones came in, Thea had them installed where the plot *should* have been."

Perhaps Penelope should have been horrified at this mismanagement, but she'd grown used to that sort of thing after a few decades in the area. "What were they fighting about?"

Esther evinced no surprise at Penelope's conversational detour. "Massimo won the jams and jellies category at the county fair with his jalapeño peach jam and Thea accused him of cheating."

"'That would do it." Penelope turned to look at the field of headstones, trying to calculate how many people would have been buried in twenty years. That wasn't a mistake that could be easily fixed, if it could be fixed at all. It meant the cemetery map was useless. "I'm surprised I haven't heard about it before. The people-buried-in-the-wrong-place thing, not the jams and jellies thing." She paused. "How do you even cheat while making jam?"

"Massimo's neighbor entered a blackberry ginger jam that was nearly identical to Thea's, which made the jalapeño peach stand out. Thea claimed Massimo had spied on her to find out what she was making, and then made the batch for the neighbor to submit."

Penelope didn't react to Zoomy peeking out from behind a gravestone two rows away. "For fair drama, that's pretty mild." It was not uncommon for brawls to break out after the vegetable judging. Amateur farmers were a passionate lot. "Is that even against the rules?"

"No. And that wasn't even the biggest drama that year. The pie table collapsed when only half the pies had been evaluated, and the judges handed out awards anyway.

There was nearly a riot." Esther smiled fondly over the memory before gesturing at the hole in the ground. "The cemetery committee knows, of course, but too many people would be hurt if they found out they've been putting flowers on a grave in the wrong spot. And it's not clear exactly how many plots are affected." She picked up the thermos nestled beside her and unscrewed the lid. "It really wouldn't be a problem at all if Elmer's grandson was spending his money on something more useful than a family mausoleum."

"True." Penelope shook the treat bag, but didn't look around.

Elmer's grandson lived three counties away and had decided that his political aims would be furthered by tangible evidence of his family's ties to the community. To achieve this, he'd erected a mausoleum in a cemetery in his district and was now working to populate it with members of his family tree. In most cases, this meant he was paying someone to dig up a grave and ship him a box of dirt; in non-stainless-steel caskets, there was usually nothing left after a decade or two.

Penelope wondered if other cemeteries had similar record-keeping deficits. If so, Elmer's grandson might as well have saved his money and picked up potting soil from the garden center. She reminded herself not to suggest this if she ever met him.

"Don't look now," Esther murmured, "but the dog is right behind you."

"Perfect." The key was not to rush things. Zoomy would be able to dart away faster than she could grab him, so she had to make him *want* to be near her. Taking one freeze-dried liver fragment from the bag, she held it at her side. A wet nose bumped against her fingers as Zoomy snagged the treat and ducked away again.

Penelope took out another treat and this time kept her hand slightly forward. Eventually, she would get Zoomy to move in front of her and he'd be stuck between her and the open grave long enough for her to get a leash on him. "So if Elmer might be anywhere, what are Derek and Matteo looking at?"

Zoomy snuck forward to grab another treat. Penelope reloaded.

Esther poured steaming tea into her cup. "I think that's a performative action so they can claim to have tried everything." She took a sip. "It might be wise to get a leash on the dog before Derek notices. He has opinions about dogs in the cemetery."

"Don't remind me." Penelope kept the treat in front of her thigh. One more treat and Zoomy should have let down his guard enough for her to grab him.

But Penelope's calculations hadn't considered Zoomy's love of treats. When he tried to eat from her hand, he knocked the freeze-dried liver away. It flew forward in a perfect arc — straight into the open grave.

"Wait, no!" Penelope clutched at the retriever, but he was too quick. The dog followed the treat into the hole, landing on the casket with a thud.

Penelope looked around innocently as Derek and Matteo glanced over at the noise.

Esther took another sip. "I suppose that's one way to catch him."

"I've always wondered what it would be like down there." As soon as the men looked back at their maps, she crouched and dropped into the hole next to the dog.

Standing on the casket put Penelope's shoulders at ground level, which gave her an interesting perspective. The grass was right in front of her eyes, and she could see the scar where the Rose Garden Society's rosebush had been grafted to hardier root stock. She could have spent ten minutes looking around from this vantage, but now was not the time to give in to curiosity. Zoomy wagged his tail as she slipped a leash over his head. "There. Consider yourself caught, naughty boy." Then she gave him two more treats.

That accomplished, Zoomy and Penelope looked up and then at each other. At least the dog had the decency to look abashed about their predicament. Penelope rubbed his neck as he leaned against her. "Esther, if I lift him out, can you hang onto the leash while I get out?"

"As long as he doesn't pull too hard."

Esther had managed entire classes of five-year-olds; she would have no trouble with one repentant Labrador retriever. Looping the leash over her wrist, Penelope adjusted her stance so the dog could use her thigh as a step. "Okay, Zoomy, up you go!"

It took two tries, with some scrabbling against the dirt of the wall and Penelope boosting the dog's rear end from below, but eventually Zoomy was on solid ground. His one attempt to run off was stopped by the leash, and then he waited happily, tail wagging, as Penelope handed the end of the leash up to Esther.

That done, Penelope considered how best to get herself back on solid ground. "Huh."

"Are you stuck?"

"Of course not," Penelope replied, offended. After a long pause, she added, "Did you happen to notice how Matteo got out?"

"He put his shoulders against one wall and walked up the other side." Esther replaced her thermos lid. "You might want to hurry. Derek is rolling up the diagrams."

"Promise you'll make Jake bail me out if I get arrested,"

Penelope said. She pressed her back against the dirt, ignoring the cold as the moisture seeped through her t-shirt. Her first attempt failed before she got both feet off the stainless steel casket.

"Of course. What's he up to today?"

The maneuver was harder than it looked. She had to maintain enough pressure against the side to keep from falling while still being able to move her legs. On her third attempt, Penelope got both feet against the dirt opposite her and began inching her feet upward. "He and Brian are house hunting," she grunted, thighs burning. "I would have gone along if you hadn't called."

Esther held up her phone and took a photo of Penelope attempting to climb out. "So Brian is serious about moving here?"

Back when Jake had been the acting police chief, Brian had been one of his best detectives and a good friend. Then Brian's marriage had disintegrated and Purcell had been hired for the permanent position of police chief. Brian had taken a job in a company out of state. After a merger and the relocation of the company's headquarters to Dubai, he was moving again.

"Looks like it. Brian's going to work for Jake part-time." Penelope's feet hit a softer section and the earth crumbled. Despite a wild scramble to maintain her place, her feet dropped back to the casket. She stood to stretch her legs. "I almost had it that time."

"Just don't damage the roots of the rosebush," Esther warned.

"I would never." Penelope brushed more dirt away from the crumbled section, hoping Esther couldn't see that part of the wall. Instead of the smooth sides that Matteo had left, she now had a tiny ledge about a foot below the ground that she could use to help push herself up. Hopefully that was lower than the rose's roots would be. Before she could try again, more dirt crumbled, revealing fabric, bright green under a layer of dirt. "Didn't the Rose Garden Society plant this?"

"Yes. Why?"

"They left a fabric weed block under it."

"What?" Esther was far more concerned about the rose-bush than Penelope being stuck in an open grave. She maneuvered her wheelchair around the side of the pit to get a better look. Zoomy followed happily behind her. "That doesn't look like any weed block I've ever seen."

Penelope tugged on the fabric, causing more dirt to crumble. "It's polyester." Which made sense, given how long it had been in the earth. Natural fibers would have degraded. Now that more of it was visible, she was able to figure out what it was. "It's a tracksuit top. Someone must have accidentally buried it when they planted the rose." Penelope routinely put down implements and then immediately lost them, so inadvertently burying an item of clothing seemed unfortunate, but completely understandable.

Esther sniffed. "Taking it out now will damage the roots."

Penelope put her back against the dirt and got one foot into the depression. The new indentation really did make it much easier to get purchase against the opposite side of the grave. Zoomy took advantage of his new position to lean forward and lick her ear.

Then Penelope's brain caught up with what her eyes were seeing. That wasn't a root sticking out of the fabric.

That was a bone.

She let her feet drop down again. "Esther, when

Massimo dug graves wherever he felt like it, how deep did he dig them?"

"Six feet. He was a stickler about that."

Penelope grimaced, and moved sideways, away from the tracksuit and the bones it contained. "We need to call the police."

That body wasn't supposed to be there.

TWO

The 911 dispatcher was new enough that she didn't recognize Penelope's voice, so it took firm insistence and escalation to a supervisor before Penelope's report of a body in the cemetery was taken seriously. Halfway through the call, Matteo and Derek arrived, but Penelope left it to Esther to explain to them what was going on.

When she'd finally been assured that a patrol car had been sent, Penelope put her phone away to find Matteo looking down at her. Without a word, he extended one calloused, muddy hand. Though she wanted to perfect the art of climbing, preferably with a few tips from Matteo, trampling the evidence probably wasn't a good choice. Besides, she really didn't want to be in the grave when the police arrived. So she took Matteo's hand and let him pull her out.

"Thank you," she said, brushing mud from her shoulder.

He nodded, picked up the wheelbarrow handles and trudged uphill with his tools. Now she understood why he often had dried mud all along the back of his shirt — one of life's little mysteries solved.

Derek broke off his conversation with Esther to turn to Penelope. "How did this happen?" He stabbed a finger at the hole in the ground.

Though she was tempted to point out that he was there when Matteo was digging down to Josephine Harper's stainless steel casket, Penelope decided that might be bad for Derek's blood pressure. "Zoomy fell in. Then I jumped down to get him out."

Anger turned to confusion. Penelope's words often caused that reaction, or at least the second part, though everything always made sense to her. But then Derek's face took on the righteous cast she'd seen more than once. "And *why* were you letting the dog run loose? There are signs posted at every entrance saying dogs are required to be leashed at all times."

There were dirt crumbles *inside* her shirt. If Esther had been the only one around, Penelope would have just taken her t-shirt off and shaken it out, but Derek would probably find some other rule to yell at her about. So she kept her shirt on and flapped the back hem instead. "You know that, and I know that, but Zoomy can't read."

"What? Who?"

Penelope brightened. There was nothing she liked more than introducing people to dogs. "This is Zoomy," she said, taking the dog's leash from Esther. "He's a Labrador who loves liver treats, belly rubs, and running away from home." That last bit was said with a frown at the unrepentant dog, who gazed adoringly at the new person, tongue hanging out the side of his mouth. "I've been trying to find him off and on for the last two days."

Derek Smith wasn't a dog lover, but only a monster would be unmoved by Zoomy's charm. Within two minutes, Derek was crouched, rubbing the dog's belly as he gave his

speech about unleashed dogs being banned inside the cemetery in a pleasant tone interspersed with comments like,
"And will the good boy remember this in the future?"

Having tracked down Zoomy multiple times in the last
two years, Penelope doubted this would be the end of the
dog's unaccompanied visits with the dead — especially now
that he'd received treats here — but Derek's optimism was
endearing. Then the first police car arrived and he was all
business again, walking down the hill to greet a male patrol
officer Penelope didn't recognize.

"You have some dirt on your cheek," Esther said.

Penelope looked at her arms, which were covered in
drying mud except for the places Zoomy had licked it off. "I
need a shower." Then she looked at Zoomy. "I forgot to call
his people."

"You do that," Esther said, "and I'll try to convince this
young man we aren't needed here any longer."

By the time Penelope had finished telling Zoomy's
owner the good news and arranged to meet her at the south
entrance of the cemetery, the patrol officer had walked up
the hill, looked into the bottom of the open grave in confusion, and been corrected by Esther, who pointed out the
jacket and bones under the rosebush. At that point, he got
on his radio, moved everyone farther away, and began
putting up crime scene tape.

"I'm not sure how much evidence they're going to find
on the ground nearby after all this time," Penelope said
doubtfully. But she said it softly enough that only Esther
would hear it. There was no point in causing confusion at
what might be this officer's first time securing the scene of a
serious crime.

"It will keep everyone else from falling into the hole,"
Esther pointed out.

Penelope looked at the grave, with the mound of dirt on one side and the rosebush on the other. "I think that's the end of that plant." Esther might know how to grow roses, but Penelope was an expert at killing them — having the police dig up the entire plant and look through the roots for evidence would do it.

"I took cuttings yesterday, just in case," Esther said, turning her wheelchair to go down the path where another police car, this one unmarked, had arrived. "I'll graft them onto the Dr. Hueys on my porch. I knew I'd need them for something."

Presumably that made sense to a gardener. Before Penelope could ask, she saw Detective Brianna Sanchez emerge from the passenger side of the car. "Oh, good. Brianna will..." She trailed off when she saw Chief Purcell get out from the other side. "Is it too late for me to hide?"

Relations between Penelope and Chief Purcell ranged from frosty to volcanic, and he'd threatened to arrest her for things entirely outside her control. More than once. The man hadn't liked dogs even *before* Penelope's mastiff, Brutus, had ruined his most expensive shoes.

Penelope didn't trust anyone who disliked dogs.

From the way his jaw bulged when he caught sight of Penelope, absence hadn't made Purcell's heart any fonder in the two weeks since they'd last seen each other at the fire department's pancake breakfast. He stomped past her and Esther with one palm held up toward them, detouring off the path to avoid Zoomy's nose.

Brianna followed more slowly, pausing to scratch Zoomy's chest. She glanced at Penelope's muddy clothes. "I take it you found the body?"

"Yes."

"I'm going to need those clothes. I'll come by later to get

a statement from the two of you. Tell the chief I said hello." For a significant portion of the police force, Jake would always be known as "the chief," another thing that irritated Purcell. "Now get going before *he* decides to keep you waiting around until the CSI team is finished."

Penelope didn't need to be told twice. She and Esther hurried down the path as Detective Sanchez resumed climbing. They reached the entrance just as Zoomy's owner drove up, and from the energy of the dog's greeting, nobody would have been able to tell that Zoomy had actively been evading her for days.

Esther's house was on the way to her own, so Penelope walked alongside, half jogging to keep up with the wheel-chair. Usually, Esther only used this speed when she was late for something. As far as Penelope knew, she'd had the entire day set aside to make sure the rosebush wasn't manhandled when Elmer's remains were being dug up. "What's the rush?"

Esther blinked and slowed the chair, confirming Penelope's guess that she'd been thinking about something else as she hurried home. "I'm sorry. It's just..." She stopped speaking and shook her head. "I need to double-check some dates in the Rose Garden Society's ledgers."

"You know who the body is," Penelope hazarded.

"Maybe. But the dates are all wrong." She frowned. "Come over when you get a chance." Then she quirked one eyebrow, and she was once again the Esther that Penelope knew. "After you get cleaned up."

Penelope checked her schedule. "It might be a few hours."

"That's fine. It will take me a bit to find what I'm looking for." Esther turned to go up the path to her house. As she went up the ramp to her front porch, she called over her shoulder, "Bring your young man along, if he's free. I have a different matter for him."

AS SHE WALKED toward her own house, Penelope texted her husband. *Brianna says hello.*

Twenty seconds after she'd sent the text, she answered the phone. "That was fast. You must be tired of looking at houses."

"So *much* beige." In the background, a woman was talking about neighbors and schools. The volume decreased when a door closed. "It's hard to look past once you notice it. Do I want to know where you ran into Brianna?"

"Extra body in the cemetery. Oh, and Zoomy's back home!"

A pause. "You okay?"

"Yeah. Muddy and a little sore from trying to climb out of a grave, but at least I didn't have to deal with Purcell."

In the ten seconds of silence that followed, she could picture Jake rubbing a hand over his face. "How did you...? Never mind. You can tell me over lunch. I'll be home in thirty minutes."

"Don't let Brian give the dog any more pizza," she said, "or he's going to be responsible for the cleanup."

"He's been warned. See you in a bit."

THREE

If Penelope had been convinced there might be useful evidence on her clothes, she wouldn't have let Brutus sniff her so thoroughly when she walked in the house. As it was, she suspected there would be far more mastiff slobber than anything else if the police ever bothered to analyze her t-shirt and shorts, though she carefully folded her clothes and put them in a paper grocery bag along with her shoes.

But having listened to many — *many* — complaints about budgets and how ridiculous the CSI shows were, Penelope knew Detective Sanchez was just being thorough. The bag with Penelope's clothes and shoes would sit on a shelf somewhere until it was either given back to her or thrown out. Back when Penelope was younger and more naïve, she would have expected to get her clothes back quickly. Now that she was older and had a better idea of how the police department worked, Penelope was glad she hadn't been wearing anything special.

When Penelope had washed all the mud from her hair — if she ever practiced getting out of a grave again, she would be sure to put her hair up under a hat — she found

Jake alone in the kitchen making grilled cheese sandwiches. Leaning in behind him, she wrapped her arms around his waist. "No Brian?"

Jake flipped a sandwich. "He offered to dig up the permits on the Yaros case." A dispute between neighbors about a shed had escalated, and now lawyers and private investigators were involved. "I think he's trying to give us some space." After a pause, he added, "Or maybe he's avoiding the dog."

At that, Brutus lifted his head from his bed in the corner of the kitchen. Brian had been staying at the house for two days, and Brutus adored him. Or possibly the dog adored the snacks that Brian unsuccessfully hid from him. Either way, Brutus had spent the previous 48 hours following his new buddy around non-stop.

As Penelope rested her head against her husband's back, she considered her schedule and whether they had enough time for her to drag him upstairs and —

"So," Jake said, interrupting her train of thought as he sprinkled more cheese on the bread. "What's this about a body?"

That broke the mood. Penelope released her husband with a sigh and turned to open the refrigerator so she could evaluate their vegetable choices. "I told you about how they were digging up Elmer, right?"

"And the Rose Garden Society was sending an observer to make sure the rose wasn't damaged," he confirmed. "I'm more curious about the part where you ended up in a grave and found an extra body."

"As you should be." Penelope recounted her morning as she heated the stir-fried cashew broccoli. It didn't really go with grilled cheese, but if they didn't eat it soon, one of them would decide that the easiest way to dispose of it was to give it to Brutus, and his broccoli flatulence could clear the house.

Jake listened attentively, only occasionally nudging Penelope back on track when she went off on a tangent. By the time she had reached the part where Purcell showed up, they were finished eating.

"How long has it been since the rosebush was planted?" Jake leaned back and gazed at the ceiling.

"Twenty years? Maybe twenty-five? Esther would know for sure." Penelope held up her index finger. "She wants to talk to you this afternoon, if you have time."

Jake looked at her. "About the body?"

"Something else. But she didn't tell me." Since there was just a bit left, Penelope divided the remaining broccoli between their plates. "It should be pretty easy to tell whose body it is if we know when it was buried. There couldn't have been *that* many people who went missing around here then, could there?"

"It was before I'd moved here, but I wouldn't have thought so," he replied. He looked at the broccoli on his plate, gave Brutus a surreptitious look, and then gave Penelope an innocent smile when he saw that she'd noticed. His attempt to pretend he hadn't been thinking about giving the vegetables to the dog failed as Brutus jumped up from his bed and came over.

Penelope narrowed her eyes at her husband and then turned to the dog. "Lie down," she said, pointing to the corner.

Brutus looked at Jake.

"Sorry, Buddy. She's the boss."

After a deep sigh, Brutus turned around and threw his bulk down on the bed. Penelope reached into her pocket, realized she didn't have any treats there, and compromised by tossing him a tiny floret from her own plate. She squinted as she looked at the mastiff. "Wow. All that extra exercise to get ready for search and rescue training is paying off. I can see actual muscles on our dog."

Then she switched her attention back to their conversation. "I was here then, but Seth was in school and I was trying to work and figure out the single mom thing, so I was a little busy." After her first husband had left to start his next family, Penelope had spent many sleepless nights trying to keep her son from feeling abandoned. But Seth had grown up into a responsible adult, so on the whole, she thought she'd done a great job. "I don't remember anyone going missing at that time, but I might not have known."

Jake eyed his plate, grimaced, and picked up his fork. "You don't know for sure that's when the body was put there, though."

Penelope considered that for a moment as she watched her husband eat. "I'm pretty sure it's not possible to dig up a big rosebush, put a person in the hole, and set the rosebush back in the ground without anyone noticing." The Rose Garden Society paid attention to that sort of thing. They definitely kept better records than the cemetery did.

"Probably not. But the body might have already been in the ground when the rosebush was planted on top of it." He balanced the last of the broccoli on his fork. "I didn't see it. Is that possible?"

Thinking back to the grave and her perfect view of the rosebush base, Penelope scrunched up her face. "Maybe? But it would be an *awfully* big coincidence that they chose to plant it directly over the body."

"That depends." He rose and took their dishes to the sink. "Did they pick a random spot, or did it replace a plant that had died?"

Penelope stared at his back. "So it could have been someone who went missing a long time ago. How long do rosebushes live?"

"When *you* take care of them? Or generally?" He snuck a glance over his shoulder, biting back a smile. "A few decades, I think. At least for the older ones."

Penelope stood up and grabbed the dishcloth. "I still think it would have been difficult to plant the new rosebush there without noticing. It just wasn't that far below ground." She leaned closer. "Missed a spot."

"That's a chip." He raised the plate and let her run her finger over the broken surface. "It's probably time to get a new set of dishes."

"Or," Penelope said, enthusiasm growing, "we could take a pottery class and make our own."

Jake rinsed the plate again and held it out. "Don't take this the wrong way, but we still have that soap out in the garage giving me nightmares."

"That was different." But as she dried the plate, Penelope remembered her difficulty following directions. Jake still had to leave the garage door open most days to keep the perfume in the soap from seeping into the house. "You may have a point. I still think it would be fun."

"Then you should definitely take a class. But in the meantime, it might be time to buy some new dishes."

"Fine. But not today. We have to find out what Esther needs to tell you first."

FOUR

Since Jake had offered to go for a run with Heidi, the German shepherd, Penelope made it through the mid-day list of pet sitting duties by three o'clock. That left three hours before she needed to start the evening rounds. She'd even dropped off her bag of clothes at the police station, where the desk sergeant promised to give them to Detective Sanchez.

Esther was on her front porch, gardening supplies laid out on the table in front of her. She glanced up when she heard Penelope's steps on the ramp. "Can you grab the isopropyl alcohol for me? It's in the front bathroom cabinet."

"Be right back." Penelope opened the door carefully, alert for Pirate, who occasionally tried to dart out the door. Even though the cat only had three legs and one eye, he could be speedy when he wanted. But Pirate wasn't waiting by the door, and Frito, the white Persian, sauntered over so Penelope could drape her over her shoulders.

By the time Penelope had located the isopropyl alcohol, all six cats were interested in what she was doing, and it took some quick work to close the cabinet door without any of the cats inside. Afterward, Frito graciously agreed to be set down on the couch so Penelope could go outside with the rubbing alcohol.

Jake was on the porch, pointing at a spot on a potted rosebush, when Penelope went back outside. He took the alcohol from her and drenched the curved knife.

"The two of you look like you're about to do surgery on that plant," Penelope joked. She leaned against a post to watch them.

"You need to sterilize your tools before doing the graft," Esther said. She seemed less distracted than she had earlier. "I think this spot will do," she commented, taking the knife from Jake.

Esther did the first graft, cutting a T shape on a branch, and then trimming a twig from the handful in the water glass before inserting it into the cut and binding the whole thing together with graft tape. "You do the next one," she told Jake, and watched carefully, occasionally correcting his movements as he grafted the remaining twigs.

"Well done," Esther said when he'd finished the last one. "We'll make a master gardener out of you yet." She checked them all over and turned her wheelchair. "Let's go inside."

Once they'd made it through the front door, all six cats converged on the people, and Frito had draped herself over Penelope's shoulders before she made it to the kitchen.

A red bound ledger rested on the kitchen table, but Esther moved it to the counter before they sat down. "I was worried I might know who it was you dug up this morning," she said to Penelope as she poured lemonade for the three of them. "But I was right. The dates don't work. We purchased that rose specifically for that spot the week before it was planted twenty-five years ago in April, and I heard from the person I'm thinking of months later."

Jake took his drink. "Who was this?"

"Brad Squires." Esther's nostrils flared, a sure sign that she disliked the person she'd named.

The name rang vague bells in Penelope's mind, as if she'd never known the man but had heard something about him. "I don't think I ever met him." Next to her, Jake shook his head.

"Lucky you," Esther said. "Brad was *not* a nice man."

Not nice could cover a lot of ground, from someone who kicked dogs to a person who blocked the handicapped ramp, but from the severity of Esther's reaction, Penelope guessed it was the former. Before she could ask for specifics, Jake said, "But you think it couldn't be him."

"No. The last time I saw him was around April, but I got a series of postcards from him over the summer, so he was still alive after that rosebush was planted."

Penelope really wanted to hear more details about this person, but Esther was right: a dead man couldn't send mail. "Do you remember anyone else who went missing around then?"

"Or possibly much earlier," Jake offered. "We know the body was there sometime before the rosebush was planted, but it could have been there longer."

"Only if whoever planted it ignored everything they knew." Esther turned and pulled a three-ring binder from the bookshelf behind her. As she leafed through it, she said, "The soil in the cemetery is almost pure clay. If you don't mix organic matter in, it doesn't drain properly. Ah, here it is." She turned the binder around to face Jake. "This is the procedure for planting bare root roses in clay soil. We haven't changed it in the last fifty years."

Penelope leaned to look, pushing Frito's white fluff out

of the way. "Twelve steps and three diagrams? Just to plant one thing? Really?"

Jake's lips twitched. "It's good that you went into pet care instead of gardening."

Esther ignored her and pointed at a diagram. "They would have dug down at *least* three feet, and then mixed in composted soil with the existing clay. From what I could see, the body was no more than two feet from the surface." She looked to Penelope for confirmation.

Penelope nodded. "If that. None of the other bodies in the cemetery have risen to the surface, so I don't think it would have moved."

The image of random bones poking up through the grass after every rain distracted her. By the time she tuned back into the conversation, Esther was talking again.

"... couldn't have been too much longer anyhow. I'm pretty sure that jacket was for the bowling league — the color is memorable. And they didn't have those too long ago."

Penelope wondered how she hadn't recognized the jacket at the time. "Oh. I'd forgotten about those. The league switched to that awful green when Seth was in middle school. Half a PTA meeting was spent complaining about it, because the league members had voted for one color, but the league president ordered the green instead."

Esther nodded. "Clinton's brother-in-law owned the print shop and his new employee thought she was purchasing two jackets for a different order, but it was actually two gross and they weren't returnable. Nearly put the print shop out of business."

"Always check the units," Penelope agreed. In her temping days, she'd accidentally left one business stocked with enough printer paper to fill the lobby.

Esther continued. "So Clinton got a deal on the league jackets *and* helped his brother-in-law out. Of course," she added thoughtfully, "his brother-in-law left his sister and ran off with that new employee two months later, so I'm not sure what lesson to take from that. Maybe 'be suspicious of any husband that doesn't fire the employee who destroys the business.' Or maybe just 'be extra careful when ordering hideous colors.'"

Penelope nodded. "The thrift stores were stuffed with those jackets when the league ordered the blue ones a few years later. It could be almost anyone buried in that spot."

"Then it's a good thing we aren't in charge of identifying the body," Jake said firmly, holding Penelope's gaze.

She smiled. "I'm sure Brianna's all over it." And that was true. Other than nearly putting her foot through the remains, Penelope had no connection. Detective Sanchez was more than capable of investigating a suspicious death that had happened twenty-five years before.

Jake squeezed her hand before he turned back to Esther. "You wanted to talk to me about something?"

"Yes." Esther closed the Rose Garden Society binder and replaced it on the table with a manila folder. "I'd like you to look into a few pet rescues for me. Are they what they claim to be? Are they financially stable? That sort of thing." She removed three brochures from the folder and passed them over to Jake. "All three accept cats and dogs for a large donation."

Penelope's stomach dropped. She put a protective hand on Frito, who was still perched on her shoulders. "What's wrong?" Esther would *never* give up her cats... unless she wasn't going to be around much longer.

Esther gave her a reassuring smile. "It's not for me. At least not at the moment. My old friend Stella is dealing with estate planning. She's decided to leave a sum to Wags Forever, with the proviso that they take her dogs. But something about the wording in that brochure bothers me. I can't put my finger on it." She shook her head. "Without solid evidence, I can't tell her she's making a mistake. And it won't matter at all if I don't offer a better alternative." She sat up straighter and looked at Jake. "So I want to hire you to look into these places." Esther narrowed her brows at Jake. "At your regular rates. No discounts."

"Of course," he replied gravely.

Jake's "regular rates" involved a sliding scale based on how necessary the investigation was, whether Jake liked the person, whether Penelope *disliked* the person, and the client's resources, but Penelope had never told Esther that. After all, Esther had been the one to convince Penelope to raise her pet sitting rates enough that she could save a bit of money, and she'd been right — Penelope's clients hadn't complained.

In a perfect world, Esther's friend Stella wouldn't need to send her pets off with strangers. "What kind of dogs are they?" Penelope asked. "Maybe I can find somewhere for them to go and avoid this completely."

Esther shook her head. "She has four horrible rat terriers that bite everyone who walks through the door. Stella loves those dogs, but trust me, they're going to be next to impossible to adopt out. That's why this rescue looks so attractive — they say the dogs would get their own miniature house with a fenced yard where they would stay for the rest of their lives."

Jake tapped the brochures against the table to straighten them. "How soon do you need this?"

For the first time in Penelope's memory, Esther suddenly looked her age. "Stella is having surgery on her leg next week, and there's a possibility she'll have to move to a long-term care facility if it doesn't go well. The dogs are boarding while she's in the hospital, so they're fine in the short term, but this may become relevant sooner than later."

Esther had reached the point in her life where the friends and acquaintances around her own age were starting to die off — Penelope had accompanied her to five funerals in the past six months. It seemed unfair to have loved ones stripped away like that, but the only alternative was to be the first one to go. Penelope selfishly hoped Esther would be around for a very long time.

Jake helped extract Frito from Penelope's hair, and they both stood to go. "I'll let you know what I find."

FIVE

Finding a body meant Penelope had a lot to consider, and she'd always found it easier to think in motion. Unfortunately, she was currently stuck. After a glance at her phone that told her Jake was on the way, Penelope frowned at the Siberian husky lying on the grass at her feet. "That's it, Koda! Tomorrow we're walking in circles around the block."

Innocent blue eyes looked back at her. Koda had a gorgeous black and white coat, and he used his good looks and stubborn personality to get away with whatever he wanted. In this case, he wanted to stay in the park for the conceivable future, and no amount of excited energy or bribery would get him moving toward home again.

Penelope had hoped this wouldn't happen, but she'd been prepared since Koda's owner had warned her this was the dog's modus operandi. Koda's owner solved the problem by lifting the dog in a fireman's carry and hauling him back home, but Penelope doubted her ability to carry the sixty-pound dog half a mile. If Jake hadn't been available, she'd have brought a cart along, but her husband had offered to pick them up in the car if necessary.

"Balto would be embarrassed by you," she informed the husky lounging at her feet. "He would never have plopped down and refused to go home." Or maybe he would have — the famous rescue mission to bring lifesaving vaccines had been one-way, after all. Perhaps refusing to turn around and go home was built into the breed.

Koda rolled and wiggled so he could scratch his back against the grass, unbothered by thoughts of Balto's approbation.

A bus full of barking dogs briefly caught his attention, but by the time the Happy Dog Day Care vehicle was at the corner, Koda had lost interest. "All those dogs spent the day hiking," she told him. "And none of *them* needed to be carried back to the bus." Her second attempt to shame him fell on deaf ears.

A sedan stopped at the curb in front of them. It wasn't Jake's car, but Penelope recognized it as an unmarked police car even before Brianna got out. A quick glance told her Chief Purcell hadn't come along, thankfully. As the detective walked toward her, Penelope said, "I left those clothes for you at the front desk."

"Thanks. I'll try to get them back to you." Detective Sanchez looked down at the dog. "What kind of sled dog refuses to walk back home?"

"You must have been talking to Jake."

"Yeah. He told me you would be here. I'll drive you back, but let me take your statement first." She sat down in the grass next to the husky and let him sniff her hand before she took out her notebook and pen. "Tell me in your own words..." She stopped, and there was the hint of a tired smile as she looked at Penelope. "I think we can skip the part about why you were in the hole in the first place as irrelevant to the current investigation. Just tell me how you found the remains. From what Matteo and Derek said, nothing was visible when they stopped digging."

"They're right. When I started, it was all still covered by dirt." Penelope remembered the perfectly straight sides of moist clay in the grave, with precise, even shovel marks. Matteo must have left boot prints on his way out, though. Penelope hadn't seen them, which meant he'd climbed out at the other end. "There wasn't a ladder, but Esther said Matteo had put his back against one side and walked up the other."

"Ah. Like going up a chimney in rock climbing."

"Maybe? I've never done any climbing." On the whole, Penelope preferred constant movement to keep in shape rather than going into a crowded gym, but she could see the appeal of going out to a deserted rock face and figuring out how to ascend. "It's harder than you'd expect."

"And you never considered asking for help." Brianna's voice stayed perfectly bland, but she'd lifted her pen away from her notebook, a sure sign this was an unofficial question.

"I was hoping to make my escape before Derek noticed I was there," Penelope admitted. "He's not a fan of dogs in the cemetery, and once he starts lecturing, it's hard to get him to stop."

Detective Sanchez nodded and moved her pen back into place. "So you didn't deliberately move the dirt in that area?" At Penelope's look of disbelief, she shrugged. "I have to ask."

"Definitely not. In fact, Esther was worried I was going to disturb the rosebush's roots, so I was trying not to mess with it."

"Did she try to stop you?"

"No, but she told me to be careful when the dirt started falling." The purpose behind Brianna's question hit Penelope then. "She didn't know there was a body there, if that's what you're asking. You can't honestly think *Esther* would be behind this!"

Brianna opened both hands in a what-else-can-I-do gesture. "I have to keep an open mind. Think of it from our perspective — the victim had a restraining order against Esther and she just happens to be the one monitoring the site so nobody gets too close to the rosebush today?"

"Against *Esther*?" Now *that* was interesting. "You already identified the body?"

Brianna flipped her notebook closed. "I suppose there's no reason not to tell you. There was a wallet and ID with the body, and we've already informed his brother and his ex-wife." She watched Penelope as she spoke, undoubtedly waiting to see if her words provoked a reaction. "Bradley Squires. He has a hole in his skull, so we have a presumptive cause of death as a gunshot wound."

"Presumptive?" Penelope relaxed into the conversational detour. "That seems pretty definitive."

"He could have been shot post-mortem," Brianna clarified. "It would be hard to prove one way or another after all this time." She tapped her notebook with the pen. "You've lived here quite a while. Did you know him?"

"Not as far as I know. The name's vaguely familiar, but I've met a lot of people." Brad Squires. That was the name Esther had brought up. But she'd said the dates didn't work. Penelope wanted to tell Brianna that, but if she revealed Esther had guessed who was buried in that spot decades ago, that would look bad.

"Esther never said anything about him?"

Penelope stared at the detective. "Today's the first time I've heard that name in at least twenty-five years." There. That wasn't a lie. "He really had a restraining order against her?"

"Yes." Brianna glanced at her again, as if expecting Penelope's face would give something away.

Suspecting Esther of murder was insane. Or was it? After a lifetime of watching people, Penelope had come to believe that *anybody* could commit murder under the right circumstances. Esther was no exception. Though if Esther had killed someone, Penelope trusted that, unlike most murderers, she would have had a really good reason.

But if Esther *had* killed someone... Would she have buried him under a rosebush? *Could* she have buried him there, physically, or would she have needed help?

Penelope hadn't known Esther as well back then — the older woman had been her son's kindergarten teacher nearly three decades ago, but it wasn't until after Seth went off to college and Penelope started pet sitting that they became close friends. Esther's arthritis had gotten worse in the last five years, but she'd been in a wheelchair since her twenties because of a spinal cord injury that had left her unable to walk any significant distance.

On the other hand, Esther was resourceful. And if the hole had already been dug for the rosebush, Esther could have transported the body using her wheelchair or even borrowed a golf cart. No, there was no physical reason Esther couldn't have buried him, and certainly nothing stopping her from shooting him.

"I don't think Esther has ever owned a gun."

"That's one thing in her favor," Brianna said. "But Mr. Squires had a registered nine millimeter, so he may have owned the weapon that killed him." She rubbed Koda's belly and climbed to her feet. "You ready for a ride back to the dog's house?"

"I'd appreciate it." Penelope hoisted the dog over her shoulder, staggered across the grass, and shoved him into the back seat of the unmarked car, where Koda was delighted to smell every inch of the upholstery. When Penelope sat in the passenger seat, she frowned. "No. I just can't see it. If Esther wanted to hide a body, she'd do it in a way it would never be found."

Brianna rubbed the spot between her eyes and then started the car. "If it were up to me, I'd count that as evidence. But Purcell is my partner on this one, and he's looking for a quick way to close the case."

"Where's Detective Peterson?" Purcell didn't normally investigate homicides. As far as Penelope knew, Purcell had never done anything other than show up at crime scenes to scowl at Penelope and put unnecessary pressure on his detectives.

"We're short on people, so Peterson's back working patrol for a while and Purcell is taking his place." Brianna waited for Penelope to give directions, then pulled into traffic.

They drove in a silence only broken by the enthusiastic snuffling in the back seat as Penelope thought about the situation from Brianna's point of view. Working for Purcell would be a nightmare. Working *with* him would be even worse. "Sorry."

"Do me a favor and talk to Esther. If she knows something, it would be better for everyone if she tells us now. And it wouldn't be a bad idea for her to get a lawyer. Purcell is pushing to have her detained and brought in for a formal interview."

"I'll talk to her." Penelope felt Koda's nose on the back of her neck. "Hey, does this car have a siren? Koda likes to sing along."

"Yes, the car has a siren, but..." Brianna was quiet for a moment. "Yeah, sure, why not? Maybe they'll fire me." She rolled down the windows and flipped a switch, and they drove the last two blocks with all three howling in harmony.

SIX

Dinner that evening was Chinese takeout that Brian had picked up after viewing yet another house, this one right around the corner. "You were right — it's a complete tear down," he said as he put the bags on the kitchen table and accepted a cold beer from Jake. "The floor's sloping toward the appliances in the kitchen and there's smoke and water damage upstairs in the main bedroom that they tried to hide behind wallpaper. I leaned on the banister and almost went through it."

Penelope put Brutus's dinner on the floor, washed her hands, and took a seat. "We could always build you a little hut in our backyard. Hiring a hermit to live in the garden was all the rage in England at one point."

"It would make for an interesting line on my resume." Brian passed her the rice.

"You know you're welcome to the guest room for as long as you want," Jake said. "Something will come up." He peered into the carton of stir-fried beef, sniffed, and drew his head back. "Extra spicy," he said as he handed it to Penelope.

"I still have a few more to look at tomorrow." Brian handed Jake an unopened carton. "This one is mild."

Brutus groaned from his bed in the corner, reminding them he was there.

Penelope glared at Brian, who had glanced toward the dog. "Don't you dare. You do *not* want to find out what happens when he eats spicy food." She turned to Jake. "Did you talk to Brianna when she came by?"

"Just enough to tell her where you were. Why?"

Penelope took a bite of the spicy beef as she considered how to phrase her concern. "You know I used to temp in offices, right? Before I started pet sitting."

Brian looked alarmed. Jake merely nodded and said, "And it continually amazes me that our downtown is still standing."

"I wasn't that bad. Mostly. But back to my point. A lot of companies employ temps because they're having a hard time retaining staff. So I've worked with a fair number of people who are one bad interaction away from lighting their desk on fire and running off to live in a Tibetan monastery. You recognize the look after a while."

Jake put down his fork. "And you think Brianna's at that point?"

"She agreed to turn on the siren so Koda could howl along when she drove us home."

Jake and Brian exchanged a long look. Finally, Brian said, "It might make fewer waves if *I* invite her out for a beer. Purcell's a little touchy about people reaching out to you." He took out his phone and started texting with one hand while eating with the other.

Having successfully passed the problem along to someone better equipped to handle it, Penelope went back to her food. "They've already identified the body. It's

Brad Squires, the guy Esther mentioned. Shot in the head."

"Brad Squires," Brian echoed, setting down his phone. "Now there's a name I haven't heard in a while. Not to speak ill of the dead, but he was a piece of... work."

Jake sat back in his chair, beer in hand. Penelope recognized his intent listening pose. "In what way?"

"He was bad news all around, but he was smart and sneaky, so we could never get him on anything." Brian shook his head. "This was back when I was working patrol, right? His neighbors called us multiple times on domestic disturbances, but each time we got there, his wife didn't have any visible bruises. She and the kid were clearly terrified, but we could never get her to leave or press charges."

Thinking of Esther, Penelope asked, "How old was the child?"

"Young. Four or five, maybe? Your friend Esther had the boy in her class. She brought in CPS, but Squires knew how to work the system. There was never anything they could point to that they could show to a judge. The wife would never talk. And he was the king of documenting situations in his favor." Brian stopped to swig his beer, the movements carefully controlled. "You've run into guys like that before," he said to Jake.

Jake nodded. "Eventually, they make mistakes, but until then, you have to walk on eggshells and document everything."

Brian nodded. "Esther kept pushing, asking questions, trying to get proof so she could help that kid, and Squires sued her for harassment. 'Look, she was on my property again' and 'She contacted my employer and tried to get me fired.' At one point, I think he took out a restraining order against her. Which was just..." He paused, glanced at Penelope, and chose a different word. "It was just garbage. But he knew the legal system and guys like that are hard to pin down."

Penelope was beginning to see why Esther had such strong feelings about Brad Squires even twenty-five years later. She was positive she'd never heard about the domestic violence, yet she'd heard *something* negative about the man. "Would anyone else have had a grudge against him?"

Brian huffed a laugh. "It would be hard to find someone who didn't, though usually the police weren't involved. Smart people avoided him if they could. Squires filed so many small claims court disputes that the judges recognized his car in the parking lot."

Penelope mixed the bland stir-fried vegetables into the spicy beef in an attempt to make them palatable. The restaurant allowed her to add extra vegetables to another dish — not an option listed on the menu — but Brian hadn't learned all their takeout secrets. "So why wasn't he reported missing? He seems like someone whose absence would be noticed, even if everyone heaved a sigh of relief because of it."

"Oh, trust me, everyone noticed," Brian said. "But we thought he'd left on his own. He worked in accounting for the parks and recreation department. They had some irregularities in the accounts and the morning of the audit, he failed to show up to work."

"Ah." Jake slid his plate over so he could transfer the crispy noodles to her plate. "That would explain it."

"Yeah." Brian quirked an eyebrow. "That can't be too spicy, even for you."

"Too much garlic. Gives me heartburn."

"Sorry. I had them add extra. Must suck to get old." Brian, who was maybe five years younger, stretched to pick up the carton and dump the rest on his plate. "Squires also had a side business, installing water softeners or something like that, and his partner had bought out his half of the business the night before. So he would have had a bunch of cash *and* a reason to skip town."

Penelope finished Jake's crispy noodles and decided if she ate any more food, she'd regret it. When she sat back, Brutus looked up expectantly. Then he dropped his head and resumed looking like he'd never been fed in his entire life. "With all that going on, why is Purcell fixating on Esther?"

Jake tilted his head slightly. "Is he?"

"That's what Brianna said." She explained about Detective Peterson being sent back to uniform and Chief Purcell taking his place as Brianna's partner.

Jake had the pained look of a man who was doing his best to stay out of a situation that he knew he could improve if he let himself get sucked back in. When he'd been the acting chief, there had been the usual problems of any workplace, but turnover had been low and he'd only rarely had to pull officers from one department to cover another. When Purcell had been hired, everyone had expected a transition period when things might be a little difficult. But it was looking like the transition period had become permanent, and that wasn't good for anyone.

"No wonder Sanchez looked like she wanted to quit." Brian grabbed his phone. "I'll call her now." He got up and went into the backyard, carefully closing the sliding door behind him before Brutus could follow him out.

As Penelope and Jake cleaned up the remains of the meal, she said, "Just so you know, I wasn't involved in the murder. Or the body dump."

He cleared his throat and attempted a serious look. "I didn't even need to ask."

"What? I could have been involved."

"I have no doubt you could have. But twenty-five years ago, we hadn't even met. If you had been involved in covering up a murder, you would never have gone out with me when I asked you."

Penelope slid against him on her way to the table. "Maybe this is my long-term plan to get away with it. Seduce the man in charge so I could guide the investigation." Then she took the dishes to the sink. "Of course, I messed up a little when I let you retire."

"No plan is perfect," he agreed.

Their gazes met and they smiled.

SEVEN

The next day, Penelope had a full roster of pet sitting clients — even with Jake helping — so she didn't have a chance to go to Esther's house until mid-morning. She found Esther filling a weekly pill organizer, "so I have my medications if they arrest me."

Penelope had texted the night before, letting her friend know about Brianna's suggestion to retain a lawyer, so she wasn't surprised to see Vivica Hammer's business card on the kitchen table when she sat down. The lawyer, known as Hammerhead to friend and foe alike, was the best criminal defense lawyer in the area. "You called her?"

"She promised to meet me at the station if I get taken in for questioning."

Penelope was relieved that her friend had hired the best, but it was also a little scary that Esther was taking this seriously. "From what Brian said, there were all sorts of people who might have wanted him dead. Why are they fixating on you?"

Esther continued inserting pills into the slots for the correct days without looking up. "They must have some reason. And there *was* a restraining order against me," she added with pride. "You'll take care of the cats?"

"Of course."

"And if I'm gone through the weekend, ask your young man to come by and water the plants." Esther looked up and gave Penelope a stern look before she could say anything. "Do *not* do it yourself. I've had some of these plants for years and I'd like them to be alive when I get back."

"This is ridiculous," Penelope protested. "They can't have evidence against you because you didn't do it." She watched Esther sort little white pills. "You *didn't*, did you? Not that I won't support you either way, but if you're going to be gone for five to ten years, it might be worth teaching me how to water those plants correctly."

"No, I did not." Esther's voice was firm. "But I don't mind obfuscating things a bit. Brad Squires was *not* a good person, and the person who killed him — whoever it was — may have had no choice." She closed her mouth with a snap and moved on to organizing the yellow pills.

Having known Esther well for many years, Penelope parsed that speech to mean that Esther thought she knew who had done it and she wanted to protect that person. Or possibly... "You feel guilty because you weren't able to protect his son from him."

Esther's hands stilled. "There must have been *something* more I could have done."

"Murder probably wasn't the answer," Penelope said, but her words lacked conviction. Maybe murder really *had* been the answer in this case. But the only person who couldn't have walked away was Brad's wife. "So you're pretty sure his wife did it."

"Hush." Esther shook out another two pills from the

bottle. "Rosella doesn't need anyone sending the police her way."

"But it might not have been her," Penelope pointed out. "Look, I trust Brianna to investigate as thoroughly as she can, but Purcell won't want to waste his budget on a twenty-five-year-old murder with an obvious suspect. If you don't want Rosella to go to prison, tell me everything you can remember. Jake and I will talk to people and pass things along to Hammerhead or Brianna."

Esther considered that as she closed the tabs on the pill organizer. "Jake needs to investigate the animal rescue. That's important."

Penelope glanced up at the ceiling for help. "Don't worry. He's got Brian looking at their annual filings, and we have a tour set up for later today." Penelope smiled. "We're prospective clients with a large trust and three pampered dogs who have *very* particular requirements. Jake is going to distract the staff with questions and I'll wander around and see what I see."

Esther smiled for the first time since Penelope had arrived. "Don't get carried away with your backstory."

"Jake talked me out of borrowing some dogs to bring along," she admitted. "We *could* bring Brutus, but nobody would believe he's a delicate soul. And it's hard to sneak around when I have to make sure he's not eating a filing cabinet."

"Brutus was not meant for undercover work," Esther agreed.

"Though he would be good at chewing up and swallowing secret notes. Now stop avoiding the subject and tell me everything you know."

As Penelope had expected, Esther had a wealth of information about multiple people connected to Brad Squires.

In the year after Brad's disappearance, Rosella Squires had divorced her husband, gone back to her maiden name of Whitmore, and sold their house. Since then, she had become an attorney specializing in family law, and now lived in a gated condominium with a full-time security guard and taught self-defense classes at the community center.

"She's taken her experiences and used them to help others," Esther said proudly.

Rosella's son, Tim, now thirty, lived three hours away and was finishing a residency in neurology.

Nearly everyone who had been working at the parks and recreation department twenty-five years ago had moved on to other things. "Some have since retired. But a few lost their jobs in the fallout after the audit revealed they were missing thousands of dollars," Esther said. "They kept it quiet, but Wayne Fauta lost his job over it. He was Brad's supervisor. Now he's the night manager at the Caribou Diner."

Penelope had been to the Caribou Diner, as had most people in the area. It was one of the few restaurants open all night, and the Mighty Moose Fries — fried potato wedges slathered in nacho cheese and topped with sliced green onions and crumbled bacon — tasted especially good at three in the morning. Penelope added jalapeños to hers and Jake ordered his without the green onions.

"Wayne? You mean *Big Wayne*? The guy with all the tattoos?"

"That's him."

After midnight on weekdays, Big Wayne was the only employee until the morning crew came in at six. When not busy in the kitchen, he sat in the booth by the door reading a stack of manga or drawing his own. Penelope had always assumed Wayne had been an artist who worked in the diner to pay his bills. One night he'd shown Penelope a neat trick for drawing eyebrows that could make a character switch from angry to excited. She couldn't imagine him at a job where he would wear a suit and tie. He'd always struck her as a peaceful soul, but physically, Big Wayne could easily have carried a body halfway across the cemetery, so he would have to go on the list of people to talk to.

"Brian mentioned that Brad had a side business? Maybe installing water softeners?"

"Not water softeners. Electric fireplace inserts. They were all the rage when they first tightened the local laws on air quality. It keeps the warmth and ambiance without causing any smoke. Or it would have if the inserts had been safer. Brad imported a knockoff version and changed the labels, though that didn't come out until later." That fall, there had been two house fires traced back to the fireplace inserts and Vincent Collins, his partner, had been forced to refund or replace all the ones that had been installed. "He declared bankruptcy. Claimed he didn't know about the switch, but at that point, he owned the entire business and was liable."

"Is Vincent Collins still in the area?"

Esther frowned. "Last I heard, he was tending bar at The Big Secret. I'm not sure he's still working there. They go through bartenders quickly."

The Big Secret was a dinner theater that survived by alternating more traditional plays with a male revue that attracted bachelorette parties and retired women's clubs. Occasionally, groups got the dates switched and couples expecting to see a semi-pro production of *Death of a Salesman* were instead treated to an enthusiastically chore-ographed medley of 70s songs with men in construction hats, boots, and very little else. Penelope had been there twice and had been glad to leave at the end of both evenings. With any luck, she could go there as soon as the doors opened, talk to the bartender, and leave before any performance started.

"Okay. His ex-wife, his boss, and his business partner. Anyone else we should talk to?"

Esther shook her head slowly. "I only know about the missing money at work and the faulty fireplace inserts because those things came out after he disappeared. If you want to know anything about his friends, you'll have to talk to his brother, Nick. He owns the body shop near the high school."

"Oh. *That* body shop. He's Brad's brother?" Penelope blew out a breath, remembering the last time she had gone to the business. "I may have to send Jake to talk to him. Seth took his car in there once and I think I'm banned from the building." She considered. "Maybe they've all forgotten about it. It's been ten years. I'm sure it's fine."

Esther gave her a knowing look. "You aren't the only one to have a bad experience there. I'd be surprised if they could remember someone they banned ten years ago, as long as you haven't been going by at regular intervals to throw rocks..." She paused, eyebrows raised.

"Nothing like that. I promise." Penelope scooped up the cats on her lap and set them on the floor. "I have to get going. I'll come by to feed everyone tonight unless I hear from you."

"Thank you."

"Good luck. If you get any prison tattoos, make sure they're spelled correctly." She patted Esther's shoulder and made her way through all the cats to the door.

EIGHT

Two hours later, Penelope stood on the sidewalk near the high school and faced the auto body shop. In one bay, she could see a young man welding under a truck on a hydraulic lift. The other bay door was closed. A hand-lettered sign above the smaller door to the left declared it to be the office. A dented tow truck sat in the otherwise empty parking lot.

Penelope gave the Catahoula by her side a treat. "I'm sure this will be fine."

Misty's startling blue eyes held some doubt, but she seemed willing to go along with Penelope's self-deception.

"We'll just go in, ask a couple questions, and then walk to the park."

Ten years was a long time to remember someone, especially at a business that saw new people every day. And Misty drew attention wherever she went, so probably nobody would look at Penelope anyhow. Yes, Penelope had a long list of suspects who *hadn't* banned her from their businesses, but Nick Squires was the only one she knew how to track down during the middle of the day. So here she was.

As she walked across the parking lot, Misty keeping pace by her knee, Penelope noticed the faded paint on the wall. "Squires Auto Body. Let us treat you like royalty." It occurred to her she might not have remembered Brad Squires at all — the negative feelings when she'd initially heard the name might have been caused by her one and only interaction with his brother's business.

A bell jangled above the door when she entered, and the smell of oil, gasoline, and dirt brought her back to the last time she'd been there. Back then, she'd been furious because her son had just been in a crash caused by a faulty repair by the mechanic. The office hadn't changed, other than the beige walls being a little dirtier and the plywood counter a little more uneven. Even similar posters were on the wall, with noir photographs of specialized auto parts next to a tiny calendar and a sales rep's contact details.

The one thing she didn't remember from the last time were the pictures taped to the wall near the computer, six in all. The people were different in each frame, but the angle was the same and all of the faces looked angry. Stills from the security camera, she realized.

Penelope forced herself to scan the pictures and found what she'd been looking for. There she was, frozen in time in grainy black and white, with a cheap black umbrella held like a club. Back then she'd been temping, so she was wearing office attire — a light-colored blouse, black slacks, and black flats. The short haircut she'd had then had been easy to style, but it had an unfortunate tendency to morph into a mad-scientist look when it rained.

It was a fairly horrifying glimpse into her past. If she leaned over the counter, she might be able to rip it off the wall and remove all traces of that outfit and hairstyle. Just in time, she remembered the security camera and grimaced, holding her ground. At least nobody would recognize her from *that* photo.

A man with an unnatural shock of black hair emerged from the room in the back, hitching up his jeans as he walked. His blue shirt with the business logo was clean and his hands showed no sign of grease or dirt. "Can I help you?"

This was Nick Squires, brother of the deceased. Penelope recognized his voice, but she would have passed him in the street without recognizing his features, though that may have been because her eye was drawn inexorably to his hair. It *had* to be dyed to achieve that color, but there was something else about the hairline that made her think he'd had work done. Ten years ago, when they'd been yelling at each other, he'd been wearing a hat.

Penelope opened her mouth to give her standard introduction, but his gaze was drawn to Misty. "That's a Catahoula leopard dog, isn't it?"

"You know your dogs." Penelope was impressed, despite her history with the man. Not many people outside Louisiana were familiar with the Catahoula breed.

"My wife and I have a purebred Pugahoula at home."

Penelope's brain stalled as she parsed that, silently damning whoever had started the nonsense naming schemes. "A pug and Catahoula mix?"

"Yeah. Except it's purebred, not a mix."

"Ah." She was here to get information about his brother. She would *not* get into an argument about dog breeds. "We were on a walk and I just wanted to stop in to express my condolences about your brother."

"Thanks. It's been kind of a shock. I thought he was on a beach somewhere and it turns out he's been dead all this time." He looked over at her and frowned. "Do I know you?"

"No." Penelope suddenly realized she had an acceptable

reason to ask questions. "But I was the one who found his body yesterday, so I feel..." She trailed off, letting him fill in the blank with an appropriate feeling. What she really felt was irritation leftover from her encounter ten years ago, but it would be better not to let him know that.

"Oh."

Okay, that wasn't really helping. She would make one last effort to get him talking about his brother and if that didn't work, she'd leave and let Jake do his man-to-man routine. "The detective who talked to me said that he'd been shot."

Nick shook his head, not in denial, but as if baffled by what went on in the world. "I loved my brother, but I can't deny he riled people up."

Penelope knew grief struck people in different ways, but this was a new one for her. If she hadn't known better, she might have assumed he was a bystander who was excited to hear the gossip. That was a little weird, but who was she to police someone's reactions, especially when that gave her an opening?

Penelope leaned in just a bit and dropped her voice. "Really? Did you tell the police?"

"Yeah, that woman detective was here yesterday. Wanted to know all about Brad's wife, and the teacher who was causing all those problems. Hell, the list of people who might have wanted to kill Brad at some point or other includes almost everyone he ever met." He snorted at that. "But you know what I don't understand?"

"What's that?"

"Well, they're saying he died in April of that year, but I was still getting postcards from him four months later! I'm not sure I trust that lady detective if she's getting something like that wrong."

"That's so weird." That was one of Penelope's stock phrases when she didn't agree with someone but didn't want to argue about it. In this case, it was true, too. Esther had also thought the timeline hadn't fit. "Are you sure the postcards were from your brother? Maybe someone else wrote them."

"No way. Nobody could fake Brad's handwriting. That's what I told that lady detective. Even dug up the postcards and gave them to her to prove it." He shook his head again and frowned at Penelope. "Are you *sure* we haven't met before? You look familiar."

Penelope waved the hand holding Misty's leash. "I just have one of those faces, I think." She backed away and reached behind her for the doorknob. "I'd better be going or we'll never get to the park." As she'd hoped, Misty heard the last two words and barked excitedly, the din painful as it echoed around the enclosed space.

Nick winced and waved her away, and Penelope escaped to the parking lot with Misty. "Good girl," she said, giving the dog another treat as they hurried away. "You're an excellent assistant. Now let's get to the park."

NINE

Running late for the visit with Jake to Wags Forever, Penelope dashed home to change. Her usual attire of shorts, t-shirts, and running shoes leaned more toward "can't be bothered to shop for clothes" rather than "rich person with pampered pets."

"Ready?" Jake called from the bottom of the stairs. "Our appointment is in ten minutes."

"We're supposed to be rich. They'll never believe it if we're considerate of other people's time," she yelled back. That rule wasn't hard and fast, of course. Their friend Tweetie's parents had enough money to run a winery, and they were two of the nicest people Penelope had ever met. But there was a little truth to the stereotype.

At the back of the wardrobe, she found the cashmere sweater her son, Seth, had given her five years before. Paired with the black slacks she wore to funerals and her black ankle boots, it gave the impression that she was an adult who didn't spill food on herself. Getting out of the house without being covered in dog hair would be impossible, but at least in their adopted personas she and Jake were *supposed* to own dogs.

"Ready!" She trotted down the stairs, boots in one hand.

Jake glanced up as he held open the front door, then deliberately closed the door and faced her, looking her up and down. "Nice sweater."

Penelope grinned as her husband moved closer. "Late for the appointment, remember?" She laughed as he herded her backward, up the stairs toward the bedroom she'd just left. "There's rich people late and then there's had to get dressed twice late."

"We could be both," Jake murmured as he nuzzled her neck, a move he *knew* made her weak in the knees.

Penelope and Jake froze as Brutus trotted to the front door expectantly.

Jake sighed, the sound barely audible over the jingling of keys on the other side of the door. "We have to find him a house soon."

Taking Penelope's hand, he led her down the stairs and then handed her the boots she'd dropped. While she sat on the step to pull them on, Jake crossed the foyer and opened the door. Brian stood on the other side, ostensibly fumbling with his key chain to pick out the house key, though the pretense would have been more believable if he'd had multiple keys that might have fit the lock. "Find out anything?"

Brian walked inside and took out the notebook he kept in his back pocket, his face suspiciously bland and not at all like he was suppressing a grin. "They have five employees and a few volunteers. Half of their expenses are from fundraising."

"Which isn't that unusual," Jake cut in.

"Agreed. But for a charity that exists in one location,

they're writing off a lot for travel and conferences. And the salaries suggest they're getting compensated pretty well." Brian staggered sideways as Brutus leaned against him. "I don't think pet care expenses would be a write-off —"

"If only," Penelope sighed. Brutus's care routinely cost more than a car payment. On a *nice* car.

Brian ignored her interruption. "Which means they're either getting a really good deal on food and vet care, or they have some small, very healthy dogs."

"Sounds like Esther was right to have reservations," Penelope said.

"Yeah." Brian moved to the side so he wasn't blocking the door. "I'll type up my findings. Have a good time."

WAGS FOREVER HAD its facility in the unincorporated area fifteen minutes from the edge of town, which gave Penelope just enough time to tell Jake everything she'd learned from Esther and relay her visit with Brad's brother, Nick. The facility's buildings were set back from the road and screened by a line of spruce trees. If Jake hadn't slowed the car to a crawl, they would have missed the tiny sign marking the turnoff onto the gravel road.

"This must be it. I hear barking," Penelope said, rolling her window down.

Beyond a gap between the trees, the driveway ended abruptly at a long, low building which left little room for parking. The place wasn't set up to handle many visitors, but maybe that made sense. After all, most of the animals would be here because their guardians had died or could no longer care for them.

Penelope glanced down at the brochure and tried to

work out the camera angle necessary to achieve the same photo. She didn't think it could be done without some trick of depth perception to make the space larger.

Jaunty vinyl letters on the single door proclaimed "Wags Forever!" Letters in a more businesslike font below stated visits were by appointment only.

"I get it," Penelope said quietly as they walked up the steps that had prevented Esther from taking the tour herself. "You wouldn't want a bunch of random people bothering the dogs, but it still feels very..." She trailed off, trying to come up with the right word.

"Controlling," Jake suggested as he tried the door. Locked. He knocked briskly, and then said in a low voice, "Don't forget. We're the Wheelers."

Penelope nodded. In her regular life, she quickly corrected anyone who assumed she had taken her husband's name after the wedding. But today they were undercover. Sort of. They'd agreed that Penelope's name was too well known in town for anonymity, and her first name was also distinct enough that she was easy to search for online. So for this visit, Jake was himself and she was Penny Wheeler — not a lie, necessarily, but definitely not the truth.

A tanned woman with auburn hair and a professional smile opened the door. Given the hint of wrinkles around her eyes, she was either a bit younger than Penelope or they were the same age and this woman had done a better job of consistently applying sunscreen. Her glossy hair with salon highlights would hide any gray, so that didn't help. "You must be the Wheelers. Welcome to Wags Forever! I'm Jessica Green. Come on in. Let me show you around."

Penelope had worked with many groups and had become pretty good at spotting the sort of people who were the backbone of any animal rescue — usually blunt to the point of rudeness, but willing to overlook most personality quirks if the other person would roll up their sleeves and help. Jessica Green didn't fit that category. She had polished manners and clothes that had never gone through a wash cycle with bleach. Then again, dressing and acting professionally wasn't a crime. It would be unfair of Penelope to hold that against the other woman.

Jessica ushered them past a mahogany desk holding a laptop, through a door into a hallway. Back here, they had chosen an epoxy resin floor, textured and colored in a grey and blue speckled pattern. Penelope lagged behind so she could crouch and run a finger along the surface. It looked easy to keep clean. She wondered if she could convince Jake to go with that if they ever redid the kitchen.

Jake cleared his throat. Penelope quit examining the floor and hurried forward to follow Jessica into a room with IV poles, a stainless steel exam table, and a glass-fronted cabinet filled with bottles. "This is our medical room, where we do regular examinations to make sure your pets are healthy. Our veterinarian comes in every month for routine care, and obviously, if there's anything more serious, we take your pet to her hospital."

Using Jake to shield herself from view, Penelope flipped the brochure over to see a woman she didn't recognize holding a stethoscope against the chest of a Dalmatian. The photo *could* have been taken in this room if it had been later repainted, since all that was visible was a beige wall and the standard exam table, but Penelope thought it might just be a stock photo. Dropping the hand holding the brochure, she stepped back into view. "Which veterinarian do you use?"

"Dr. Marsh over at East Village Vet. Do you know her? She's very good."

Penelope decided that Penny Wheeler was an exclaimer. "Ooh, I've heard good things about her." In her pet sitting business, emergencies involving her clients weren't common, but they happened often enough that she'd been to every veterinary hospital in the area. She'd met Dr. Marsh a few times over the years — the latest was when Brutus had gotten his toenail caught on something and partially torn it. From the way he'd been limping, Penelope would have sworn he'd broken his leg, but Dr. Marsh had sympathized with him, clipped off the painful nail, and bandaged it up before he'd finished sniffing around the floor to see if anyone had dropped any treats.

Having Dr. Marsh handle the medical care for the animals at Wags Forever suggested a good level of care, but East Village Vet was a bustling practice and Dr. Marsh was in demand. Penelope was surprised she had time to spend one morning a month at the rescue.

Jessica guided them back into the hallway. "And over *here* we have our three cat rooms — you can see through the windows that they have everything they need. But if I remember correctly, you only had dogs?"

"Three Pomeranians," Jake confirmed.

Penelope slanted him a questioning look behind Jessica's back. Granted, having one mastiff was more than enough for any house, but were they really Pomeranian people? Hm. Perhaps the Wheelers with money were. She adjusted her backstory and squared her shoulders.

In the room they were passing, half a dozen cats lounged on beds and cat trees while a teenage girl wearing a pink Wags Forever t-shirt scooped a litter box in the corner. The teenager didn't look up, likely because her headphones had kept her from hearing them.

Jessica waved her arm at a tiny room across the hall.

"Here we have our kitchen, where we prepare special diets for all the animals."

Penelope looked in to see a refrigerator, stacked bins of kibble with hand labels, and rows of canned food. It had the perfect look to post on social media: everything clean, organized, and very new looking. However, there wasn't enough food to get Brutus through a week. True, most dogs were smaller than a mastiff, but surely a facility like this would buy in bulk. Would Penny Wheeler, wealthy owner of three Pomeranians, notice that? Penelope decided Penny volunteered during her copious free time. "Wow, it's so organized!" She ignored Jake's raised brow at the enthusiasm in her voice. "At the county shelter where I volunteer, they have two sheds with bags of food just *tossed* inside. But I guess they have more dogs to feed..." She let her voice trail off doubtfully.

"Oh, we have more in the auxiliary building," Jessica said easily as she urged them past the kitchen, leaving Penelope to wonder about the difference between a shed and an auxiliary building. Probably how much it cost to build, she decided.

"And then outside..." Jessica opened a door on the right, letting them into the area on the opposite side of the building to where they'd come in. "We have all the dog houses."

By houses, Wags Forever meant literal houses. Each kennel was surrounded by a picket fence, with a patch of green grass and a structure that looked exactly like a house with a sliding glass door and a low couch visible within. A pet door allowed the dogs to go in or out, even when the glass slider was closed.

The houses looked smaller than they had in the brochure, but still snug and cozy. An elderly chihuahua tottered to the front of his pen and lifted a leg against the gate near Penelope's foot.

A wide paved path meandered into the distance, but with the stands of bamboo blocking her sightline, Penelope could only see the nearest five pens, though she could hear dozens of excited dogs barking beyond that. The result made it seem like a tiny cozy community, but it would be harder to keep an eye on the dogs. Then she walked a little farther down the path and noticed the security cameras mounted on light poles where the path forked.

"Mrs. Wheeler! Penny!" Jessica called behind her.

Penelope belatedly realized she was being hailed. She plastered a smile on her face and turned around. "Sorry! Got distracted."

"Not all the dogs are safe with people, which is one reason they're with us," Jessica explained, ushering Penelope toward the first pen. "Each dog gets time in the larger exercise pen every day, and the volunteers come out to sit with them so they never get lonely." She pointed to the end of the row. "We have forty houses built now, but we only have space for another ten, so we encourage people to reserve space as soon as possible," Jessica said. "If you want a closer look, we can go in this one. Muggles is friendly."

Muggles turned out to be a knee-height snub-nosed black, white, and brown dog with brown eyes. On any other day, Penelope might have missed the connection, but the ridiculous conversation she'd had with Nick Squires was still in her head. "Is that a Pugahoula?"

The last word was difficult to get out with a straight face. Jake's head tilted, just like Penelope's favorite Rottweiler when someone told her to sit and didn't immediately offer a treat, as if he wasn't sure he'd heard her correctly. Penelope's feelings about designer dog breeds were well known. If there were two Pugahoulas in the area, someone local was probably breeding them, and she suspected she would find out in the next few years whether the Catahoula genes would protect the dogs' eyes and airway, or if the pug issues would dominate.

Jessica's fixed smile increased. "Why yes it *is*! You certainly know your stuff. Muggles's owner ended up in a retirement home that doesn't allow dogs and none of his children stepped up, so Muggles lives here now." Her voice held the tone that newscasters used when describing a previous tragedy that led to the current heartwarming clip.

"Poor guy." Leaning down, Penelope rubbed Muggles's chin, which incidentally gave her a glimpse of his teeth. Though they weren't perfectly aligned — undoubtedly a holdover of his pug heritage — Muggles's teeth were blindingly white. This dog was no more than a year old, if that.

"As you can see, he has a couple of beds and a sofa where the volunteers sit with him." Jessica paused to straighten a blanket and fluff a pillow. The space wasn't large, but it was impressively fresh-smelling. "We close it up when the weather's bad, but he has the dog door and he can go in and out as he pleases."

"Gosh, it's a beautiful setup," Penelope said. "And the dogs stay here for the rest of their lives?"

"Yes. That's why we require such a large donation when we accept new animals. We need to ensure the financial security of Wags Forever, since we don't know what each pet will need in the future." She herded them out of the little house, across the grass, and out the picket fence that surrounded Muggles's area. "Can I answer any other questions for you?"

Penelope had a score of questions, but she didn't trust

Jessica to give her truthful answers. So instead, she and Jake made a show of checking with each other.

"Thank you for your time," Jake said as they walked back through the building, past the cat rooms and the medical room to the office.

"Of course," Jessica said, holding the outer door for them. "If you *do* have any questions, you know how to reach me. I look forward to hearing from you."

Knowing that Jessica could see them and would almost certainly be watching, Penelope walked demurely to the car and let Jake open her door for her. Neither said a word until they were beyond the wall of spruces and back on the road heading home.

TEN

Jake spoke first. "Pugahoula? Really?"

"Purebred, even," she said, nodding sagely. "You first. What did you see?"

"The building has so many code violations — starting with a lack of exits and windows too small to make it through in a fire — that any inspector would force them to tear it down. That says they aren't being monitored by any agency, which is a red flag."

He slowed to let a tractor cross in front of them. "Plus, they're too far out to be on the city sewer system, which means they must have a septic tank. Where is it? The way the property boundaries are set, it has to be either under the parking area or they've built a structure over it. Again, that's a code violation. If the county inspector ever does show up, what are they going to do with the animals when the buildings are condemned?"

Craning her neck to look back, Penelope asked, "How far back do you think that property extends?"

"Hard to tell with the way they've landscaped it. Why?"

"Because we never did see the 'auxiliary building',

which I think is just a fancy way of saying they have a shed. So it has to be somewhere beyond the dog runs. Which would be fine if it held tools or stuff they only used every once in a while, but it would be *really* inconvenient if you were unloading a pallet of food from a truck."

"You think there's another entrance to the property." Jake slowed to turn left at the next intersection.

"I think I'd like to take a better look around without Jessica watching." Penelope thought about it as they turned again and headed away from town on the road parallel to the one with the Wags Forever main entrance. "It's all very pretty, but *impractical*. With that many animals, they must have a dumpster to take away the waste, so where is it? Something's not adding up."

They were passing agricultural fields interspersed with isolated houses and small businesses that either didn't rely on foot traffic or needed a location far enough from their neighbors that excessive noise wouldn't be a problem. Penelope noted a shop advertising custom metal fabrication, a tractor repair service, and an emu farm.

She stared at the odd-looking birds clustered near the fence watching cars go by. "Do you think — ?"

"No, we can't have an emu in city limits." Jake slowed the car and pulled onto the dirt shoulder. "We should be just about even with Wags Forever."

Penelope ignored the emus that were now wandering over to check out the car near their fence and leaned toward her husband so she could see across the asphalt. A dirt path ran toward a house set back from the road, and next to it, a gravel lane snaked between two oak trees to an old barn. A faded sign announced discounts for group riding lessons, but half the planks around the arena between the barn and the road were missing. The arena itself was choked with weeds.

Given the terrain and the trees, they wouldn't be able to ascertain they were anywhere near Wags Forever without driving down one of the private roads or getting out of the car and trespassing on foot. What they *needed* was a view from above — except Penelope had told Jake just three weeks before that they had no need for the remote control quadcopter that had been on sale at the local electronics store. Now they'd have to drive back to town to buy it, and it probably wasn't on sale anymore.

"Ugh." Penelope drew back so she could see Jake's face, which was a study of innocence. "You're going to make me say it, aren't you?"

"I have no idea what you're talking about," he said with a pleasant smile.

Scowling at her husband, Penelope inhaled deeply. "Fine. You were right. We should have bought the quad-copter when it was on sale."

He cupped one hand behind his ear. "Sorry, what was that?"

"Oh no. You get to hear it once and only once." She paused and considered. "At least until the next time."

"Just checking." He reached down and touched the button to pop the trunk.

It took just an instant for Penelope to guess what he was doing. "Hang on." She put out a hand to keep him in place. "You don't get to claim the moral high ground when you've built your glass house in the moral canyon."

Jake lifted her hand to his lips. "Too late. You already admitted I was right."

"I take it back!"

When traffic was clear and he could open his door, Jake

slid out and walked to the back of the car. Penelope had meant to cross her arms in a pantomime of a fuming spouse, but the emus had gained enough courage to stick their necks over the fence and the scene distracted her long before Jake set something on the dirt in front of the vehicle and got back inside the car.

Penelope squinted at the screen on the control box, admiring the effortless ease with which Jake piloted the quadcopter into the air and across the road. Then she realized he knew the layout of all the controls a little *too* well. "This isn't the first time you've used this."

Jake glanced at her, and then quickly back at the screen where the quadcopter was flying over the edge of the road leading to the barn. "Well, no. Brian and I have taken it out a few times."

They would have had to do so somewhere other than near the house, because Brutus loved chasing quadcopters and the dog would have destroyed it — and probably eaten a chunk or two — when it landed. Then another thought occurred. "*That's* why Brutus is so tired when you both come back from running," she said indignantly. "You didn't train Brutus to run next to you. You let Brutus run after the quadcopter!"

"We've been going to the track," Jake confirmed. "The big guy is up to half a mile before he has to take a break."

"That's cheating!"

"No, it's not." Jake stopped the quadcopter's forward motion and skimmed over the roof of the barn, pausing on areas where the corrugated steel roofing panels were either missing or loose. "Going to be a job replacing those." He let the quadcopter move forward again. "I run and Brutus runs. We're just running at different spots. You know what he's like when you try to run next to him."

Penelope *did* know what Brutus was like on a leash. Though he was better now than when they'd first adopted him, he didn't think twice about dashing to something interesting on the other side of the path. Penelope had been knocked over a few times and once flipped over Brutus's back before finally deciding it was safer to walk than jog with him.

"So, are you planning to pilot the quadcopter in front of you during search and rescue missions?"

"We'll burn that bridge when we get to it."

Abandoning the barn, Jake took the quadcopter up higher, giving them a view of a larger area. Behind the barn, someone had converted two dozen pipe stalls of the former stables into dog runs. Each pen was covered in artificial turf and had one roofed corner to provide protection from the sun or rain. They were certainly large enough for the dogs to move around, but there were no toys or anything for enrichment. All the pens had dogs in them, most looking up at the sky toward the quadcopter.

Jake piloted the craft further back from the road. Beyond the dog runs, the picturesque dog cottages of Wags Forever began. He took it up higher so the entire area was visible. The paved walkway that ran between the dog homes of Wags Forever continued on through the former stables and ended next to the decrepit barn, where a golf cart waited.

A bus parked behind the barn caught her eye and she stabbed a finger at the screen. "Is that the...? Can you go lower so we can see the side?"

As the quadcopter swooped down, the familiar logo of Happy Dog Day Care came into view on the side of the bus.

Penelope's nostrils flared. "Hang on. They make a big

deal about how they go for hikes and group play dates, and all they do is drive out here and dump the dogs in individual dog runs for the day? That's just wrong."

"Arguably fraudulent," Jake agreed. "And also extremely lucrative."

Though she felt like growling, Penelope forced herself to watch the screen as Jake piloted the craft higher again. "Jessica said there were forty dog houses built. I only see five."

"There's no room to build fifty of them," Jake said. "Unless they're planning on buying neighboring property. Or demolishing the dog pens from the day care."

No wonder Jessica had been so anxious to call Penelope back when she'd wandered down the path. If Penelope had gone any farther, she would have seen the boundary between the tiny houses and the decidedly less attractive converted pipe stalls.

They watched as the quadcopter moved over the five dog houses and descended. A familiar golden retriever looked up, wagging her tail so hard the back half of her body curved.

"That's Betty Boop! She's not part of Wags Forever." Penelope had seen the retriever with her owner — a young woman who worked in advertising — just two days before at the dog park.

Jake slowly moved past another house, where a brown and white pit bull lay on his back in the sun, ignoring the quadcopter.

"That's Bartholomew! I haven't seen his owners in a few weeks, but they looked pretty healthy then. I doubt Bartholomew is part of Wags Forever, either. Do *any* of those dogs actually live there?"

"The good news is that they won't have to find temporary homes for all the dogs when the county inspector shuts the facility for all the building violations." After another moment, during which Jake navigated around the facility, he added, "They're probably using the houses to handle overflow from the day care business."

"Or they staged the area with a few dogs because they knew we were coming for a tour."

Jake glanced over at her. "We could ask the owners of Betty Boop and Bartholomew."

"Yes, we *could*." Penelope nodded.

The silence in the car lengthened.

"Ah." Jake coughed. "If only you knew their names..."

Penelope slumped against the seat belt. "You know how I am. There's just not enough room in my brain to remember names of pets *and* their people. So I just remember the important part."

If they had been *clients*, she'd have been able to track them down — she'd insisted on being able to search the database for a pet's name when Seth and Jake had set up everything. But with random people at the dog park, she couldn't even ask Esther who they might be based on first names.

Jake's lips twitched. "I guess I should be glad we didn't get Brutus until after you had committed my name to memory."

"Count your lucky stars." She reached out and met his hand halfway. "I might know the name of one owner."

"Let me guess. The Pugahoula."

"Nick Squires and his wife own one. I thought this one was the sign there was a new trend, but now I think this might be the same dog. But you're going to have to leave me out of it. Nick is eventually going to figure out where he knows me from, even after ten years."

"You're unforgettable," Jake said, squeezing her fingers. "I'll talk to him."

On the screen, a person walked up the path, shading her eyes with one hand as she looked up at the quadcopter. Jessica Green. "Uh oh."

"Not a problem," Jake said, easily guiding the quad-copter higher and over the neighboring property. "This can fly faster than she can run."

"Well, yes," Penelope admitted as she watched the ground whizz by under the quadcopter, "but won't she figure it out? We were just there."

The high-pitched whine of the returning quadcopter could be heard through the window, and on-screen, the car was visible.

"No, Jake and Penny Wheeler, potential clients in their fifties, were there. They didn't look like people who would be flying a drone."

Penelope looked down at herself. "Good point." But she noticed Jake didn't waste any time loading the drone into the car and driving away.

ELEVEN

When they arrived home, they went into the backyard, where Jake wrestled with Brutus while Penelope told Brian about the visit to Wags Forever.

"So how many dogs were there that you *didn't* recognize?" Brian asked as he and Penelope watched Brutus knock Jake to the ground for the third time.

"Maybe four? The cats could all be legit — I didn't recognize any of them, though I probably wouldn't." She leaned to the side to let Brutus run by. "Let me know if you need any help over there."

"No, no, I'm fine." Jake climbed to his feet just in time for Brutus to plow into him at full speed. They went down in a tangle of limbs, both of them making happy growling noises.

Brian looked at his notebook. "Given their income over the last five years..." He stopped. "It all depends on how long the dogs live. Do they make actuarial tables for dogs?"

Penelope had only the vaguest idea of what an actuarial table was used for, but she could answer the underlying question. "Little dogs live longer than big dogs. And you'd need to know how old they were when they got there. But if they're reporting five full-time employees, I would think they'd have more than four dogs."

From under Brutus's bulk, Jake said, "Which begs the question of what happened to the rest of them?" He crawled out from under the mastiff. "Though, for our purposes, it doesn't really matter. I think we can say there are enough red flags that Esther's friend should choose a different dog retirement home."

Penelope frowned. "It would still be good to find out. And I think I know how. But in the meantime, I have to go walk a few dogs and learn how to protect myself."

OVER THE YEARS, Penelope had considered taking self-defense classes, but she'd never thought about it long enough to follow through. So she wasn't sure what to expect when she showed up at the community center for Rosella Whitmore's drop-in class. It was being held in one of the group meeting rooms, with twenty chairs pushed back against the walls to leave an empty space in the middle.

Penelope had intended to get there at the beginning of class, but searching for a cat inside a house for half an hour threw off her schedule, and she arrived just in time to see two women yell self-consciously and fend off slow motion attacks from their other two classmates.

The petite, dark-haired woman on the edge of the room stepped forward and clapped once to get everyone's attention. She was wearing a narrow knee-length black skirt, low heels, and a bright red blouse — not the ensemble Penelope had expected of a self-defense instructor. Though it made sense when she thought about it; an attack didn't happen only when a person was conveniently dressed for it.

"Good job! Remember, when you're kicking, you don't need to aim for the knee. Raking the shin hurts. Stomping on the top of the foot causes a lot of pain, and it works especially well if you're wearing hard-soled shoes." She checked her watch. "You did really well today. Enjoy the rest of your evening."

The four women thanked her and grabbed their belongings. Penelope waited by the door for Rosella Whitmore, previously Rosella Squires, to answer a question from a participant. Finally, it was just Penelope and Rosella.

"Did you have a question about the class?" Rosella flipped off the lights and closed the door behind them.

"You're Rosella Whitmore, right? I just wanted to talk about your ex-husband. If now's not a good time, I can meet you later..." Penelope trailed off as Rosella's face went from friendly to guarded.

"Sorry, I'm not talking to journalists. Though I guess I should thank you for not interrupting my class." Rosella strode briskly down the hallway toward the community center entrance, her heels clicking on the linoleum.

Penelope had to trot a few steps to catch up. "No, I'm not a reporter. I'm a friend of Esther. Your son's kindergarten teacher."

Rosella's steps slowed, and then she turned to face Penelope. "Did something happen to her?"

"She's fine. Or, I think she is. The police are questioning her about your ex-husband's death, and I'm trying to find proof it wasn't her."

"They're questioning *Esther*?" Her bewilderment turned to understanding. "The restraining order."

"Yes. And I think there must be something else as well,

something they aren't telling us. But I know Esther didn't do it." When faint frown lines appeared on Rosella's face, Penelope shook her head. "Esther was there when I found the body. If she'd known it was there, she would have made sure I wasn't anywhere near it."

Rosella regarded Penelope for a moment and then seemed to come to some decision. "Let's find somewhere to sit down so we can talk."

They ended up back in the classroom, seated on two plastic chairs near the door. Rosella put her briefcase and suit jacket on another chair. "I wish I could say that Esther made me realize my own worth, and that made me leave my marriage. The truth is, Brad packed up and left on his own. But Esther tried so hard to keep Tim safe when I couldn't. I owe her *everything* for that." She folded her hands and squared her shoulders, as if bracing for a physical blow. "What do you need to know?"

Penelope didn't want to bring back painful memories, but she couldn't afford to be gentle. "Tell me about the last time you saw Brad."

Rosella's voice was soft but steady. "It was the first week in April, on Monday night. He came home from work in a strange mood." She stopped and looked straight into Penelope's eyes. "Back then, his moods were the most important thing in my world. When he was happy, things were good. When he wasn't..."

Penelope nodded. "I understand."

"So when he came home from work, I took Tim to the park until I had to get home to make dinner, because that was safer for both of us. When we got back, Brad's car was gone and so was his overnight bag."

"Was it unusual for him to just leave like that?" Rosella

had never reported Brad missing. But then again, she and her son had clearly been better off without him.

"A little, but only because he hadn't been talking about a trip. He and his friends would sometimes go to Mexico or Las Vegas for a few days, so I thought he'd be back. At least until people from his work started showing up the next day and I heard about the audit."

"And you're sure he was the one who packed his overnight bag?" Penelope thought a wife, especially one whose safety depended upon keeping Brad happy, would know what he normally took with him.

"One hundred percent. He took his favorite clothes and his passport, which he normally kept hidden in the bottom dresser drawer." Rosella shook her head. "But I don't see why everyone is so fixated on the night he left. He *couldn't* have died then."

Penelope leaned forward. "You saw him again?"

"No, but I kept getting notes from him for months." Rosella unlatched her briefcase and took out a tablet. "When I finally got brave enough to contact a divorce lawyer, she had me document all contact. I advise the same thing for my own clients now — it's usually a recording or at least notes of conversations. He was still in town." She extended the tablet so Penelope could see the screen.

Penelope swiped through multiple images of postcards, most with wording that might be completely innocuous from one person but a veiled threat coming from another. *I like when you wear that green dress for me,* said one. Another said, *Nice haircut.* All were simply signed "Brad" and were undated aside from the postmark.

"And they matched with what you were doing?"

Rosella nodded. "I hadn't worn that outfit for *months,*

but I wanted something dressier for back-to-school night. Two days later, that postcard showed up."

"That's his handwriting?"

"Yes. My lawyer even sent one to a lab because we needed to make sure he couldn't claim I'd written them myself. His fingerprints were all over it. The whole thing was a nightmare because by that time they'd realized he'd embezzled from the city and the cops kept showing up to search the house, thinking I was hiding him there. Meanwhile, I was terrified he would take Tim away." Even now, after twenty-five years — and knowing her ex-husband was dead — Rosella's hands clenched into fists.

Penelope let the silence lengthen to give Rosella a chance to breathe. After a moment, she asked, "Do you know when the last one was sent?"

Rosella took the tablet and rapidly swiped to the side. "The 28th of October." She handed the tablet over again.

This time, the postcard said, *Don't dress my son in girly costumes again if you know what's good for you.*

Anger laced Rosella's voice. "Tim wanted to be a court jester. The costume was gender neutral, not that it even mattered, and everyone at the school parade loved it. But I was too afraid to let him wear it out of the house for the neighborhood parties after that."

Assuming that was true and Rosella hadn't somehow faked the pictures, Brad Squires had been alive months after the cemetery rosebush had been planted.

And yet... nobody had noticed the rosebush being dug up and replanted with a body underneath.

TWELVE

To Penelope's amazement, the parking lot of The Big Secret was nearly full when she arrived. That was unusual for the town's perpetually struggling dinner theater and male revue. Though tempted to assume it was due to an unusually large bachelorette party, the groups of under-eighteen high school kids going through the front doors interspersed with older patrons told her this had to be a dinner theater night.

Jake got out of his car and crossed the lot to stand at her side. "What am I missing? The last time the building was this full was when we rented it out for emergency services coordination training."

Laughter bubbled up. "That's right. I forgot that was *here.*" Training Con One had occurred before they had started dating. Penelope had been hired to play a victim of a natural disaster, which had gone well until she'd gotten bored. In retrospect, she should have realized that a job lying around with fake blood all over her shirt and hair was a terrible fit, but the money had been good.

Jake snaked an arm around her waist. "It was good

training for everyone to know that people sometimes act irrationally at mass casualty events." He smiled. "The first time I saw you, three firefighters were offering bribes for you to come down from the catwalk."

"And you thought, now *there's* the woman I want to marry," Penelope supplied.

Jake turned a strangled laugh into a cough. "Something like that."

"They should have told me they were being graded on how quickly they got all the injured people out of the building," she said indignantly. "And it wasn't *my* fault the other victims realized they were missing out."

"Many lessons were learned that day," Jake agreed.

There had not been a Training Con Two. At least, not one that had hired amateur actors.

"In my defense, I was left unsupervised for a really long time." Penelope leaned against him. "I'm thinking about using that as my epitaph. Except they don't really allow big gravestones anymore, do they?" With a frown for the end of such a useful tradition, she stood up straighter. "Ready?"

The Big Secret had two separate public areas: in the back was the theater, a huge room big enough to hold sixteen round tables and a raised stage along one wall; and in the front was the bar. For both theater and revue nights, the bar was a place to get away from whatever was happening on stage or between the tables, and it often held more people than the theater.

Event tickets were checked at the door between the two — the theater's owner had hoped to add "local bar" to the list of the building's attractions, but even with the doors between the sections closed, everything could be heard in the bar area. Not many people wanted to listen to shouted dialogue, random cheers, and the same ten songs every other night. There were more convivial places to drink.

As they went through the main doors, Penelope was hit by a gust of humid air that smelled like fry oil and ketchup and, underneath it all, a hint of moldy carpet. "They wanted me to lie down on that floor," she whispered to Jake.

"Oh, the horror," he whispered back.

A group of laughing teens had queued up to go into the theater, phones raised to show digital tickets. Other than that, the front area was empty aside from the man behind a polished pine bar at one end of the room. Somehow, it felt like a backstage area with the cacophony of patrons talking on the other side of the wall.

The bartender was a slim white man, possibly in his late forties, though Penelope found it hard to reliably guess ages of people younger than herself... which now included a significant portion of the population when she wasn't standing in a retirement home. He was currently mixing drinks and placing them on a tray, presumably for a server to take into the theater.

Jake nudged her elbow. "Did you see this?"

Tacked to the wall was the poster for the current shows. Tonight's play was *Steel Magnolias*, and for a moment, Penelope was tempted to buy a ticket just to find out the extent to which a southern accent could be butchered by off-off-off-Broadway actors. Then she realized the title had been altered. "Steel-*toed* Magnolias?"

"A gender-swapped re-imagining," Jake read slowly. "'That's probably so they don't have to pay licensing fees."

Penelope had to squint to read the smaller type. "A group of construction workers gather at their favorite coffee shop to help each other through life's challenges and joys." She regarded the rest of the poster. "Huh. Well. That's certainly a thing." Esther had helped her come up with that line.

Jake pointed to the last row of text. "Written by Vincent Collins & Steph Teller."

Penelope glanced at the bartender. "Esther would understand if we came back later to question Vincent Collins, right? We could have dinner here and watch the show."

"Focus. We already have plans to eat at the diner later." Jake took her arm and they walked to the bar.

The bartender looked up at their approach, but didn't stop pouring. "Howdy, folks. What can I get you?"

Before Penelope could say that they just wanted information, Jake said, "Two lime and tonics, please."

"Coming right up." He set his final drink on the full tray and set up two fresh glasses with quick, sure movements.

Penelope hopped up to sit on the bar stool. "You're Vincent Collins, right?"

"For my sins. You here for the show?"

"Not really," Penelope said, "but now that we know it exists, we'll be back."

A smile creased the bartender's face, and he looked up as he set two clear drinks on napkins in front of them. "Ridiculous, isn't it? But the cast and crew formed a collective last spring and we bought the owner out. To make a go of it, we needed to bring costs down, so Steph and I offered to write something. We didn't have a costume budget, but we had construction worker outfits from the male revue. And thus, Steel-toed Magnolias was born."

Jake tucked a large bill into the tip jar and picked up his drink. "It's inventive."

"It's horrible, is what it is," Vincent said with a good-natured grin. "But it's so bad that it's good, if you know what

I mean, and the kids have nowhere else to go. They come back and bring their friends. It's sort of real-life viral." He handed off the tray to a server in black jeans and a pink t-shirt and started on the next ticket. "Plus, we stopped trying to cook our own food and just order from the fast-food chains in the area instead, so the rat problem has gone away. The place is finally making a decent profit. The previous owner is spitting nails, but he's only got himself to blame. He ignored our suggestions and kept trying to stage *Don Quixote* accompanied by overcooked pasta."

Penelope nodded. "I'd rather see *Steel-toed Magnolias* than *Don Quixote*."

"You aren't the only one." Vincent reached behind him to pick a bottle from the rack. "I assume you're here to talk about Brad." He saw Penelope's guilty look and gave an easy laugh. "You're not here for the show and you know my name. And Brad's body being found is the only interesting thing that's happened around here all week."

Penelope was encouraged by his good humor. "Do you mind talking about him?"

"It's fine. I've already talked to the police and I've felt like an idiot for twenty-five years, so there's no point in trying to hide things now." He took a deep breath and let it out slowly, all without slowing his hands. "I've worked on getting more zen about it over the years."

"You had a business with Brad," Penelope prompted.

"We had an unregistered and unlicensed business," Vincent corrected, "a fact which only became obvious to me later. I met Brad when I was working part-time doing main-tenance for parks and rec. Somehow, he found out I'd just inherited some money from my aunt. He had some connec-tion who had a bunch of fireplace inserts for cheap, and Brad didn't have enough cash for the full shipment or time to install them all, so we both ponied up half the amount and called ourselves the Cozy Fireplace Guys."

"When was this?" Jake asked.

"About six months before he skipped town."

Vincent handed the full tray off to the same server just as a woman's slightly muffled voice came through the wall. "Welcome, friends! For those who haven't been here before, The Big Secret is dinner theater of a different kind. Now sit back, relax, and enjoy *Steel-toed Magnolias*." Whistling and clapping greeted the end of her introduction, but it quieted quickly, only to come back again as the first character entered the stage.

From Jake's pained sigh, he had just realized they were coming back to watch the show someday soon.

Vincent continued. "I figured out pretty quickly that it was a mistake to be in business with the guy. He could find customers, but it was up to me to make them happy, which was nearly impossible because he would promise all kinds of things. I did most of the installations, or at least, I thought I did, so we didn't interact much. But it got to where we couldn't be in the same room without it turning into a shouting match."

"So you split up the business," Penelope said. The bubbles in her water tickled her nose, but the lime was a nice touch.

"It was his idea," Vincent said, still pouring drinks as he spoke. "All I needed to do was pay him for his half of the remaining units, and then I'd have the business name, the customer lists, the storage unit, everything."

"That *seems* reasonable," Jake said, but he let the words lengthen, as if he knew there was something that hadn't worked out.

"Yeah, but it turned out he'd done some installations on

his own and pocketed the money," Vincent said. "Which meant I paid him for units we no longer had. Then, when I found out about the recall, I contacted all our customers."

"Except there were customers you didn't know about," Penelope said, thinking of the house fires.

"I'm just grateful nobody was hurt," Vincent said. For the first time, his hands stilled, but only for a few seconds. Then the smell of coconut permeated the air as he mixed another drink. "With the way the business was structured — or rather, not structured — I was personally liable, because the business name was on the paperwork and I owned the business." He slotted the bottle back in place, put the last glass on the tray, and leaned his elbows against the bar. "So I had a bunch of great reasons to kill Brad. Fortunately for me, the last time I saw him, I hadn't learned about them yet."

Jake nodded. "When was that?"

Vincent looked at the ceiling as if searching for his calendar. "The police asked me that and I couldn't say. But I've been thinking about it all afternoon. It would have been a Monday night because I couldn't get the cash from the bank until Monday. We met in the evening at my place. I gave him the cash, he signed everything over to me, and I never saw him again."

Having interviewed other people connected to Brad Squires, Penelope had a good idea of what happened next. "Never saw him again," she repeated, "but it wasn't the last you heard from him, was it?"

"No." Vincent picked up a knife and began slicing lemons with more force than necessary. "We had a cold snap in August, enough that people started using the inserts, and one of them shorted and nearly started a fire. Two days later, I got a postcard from Brad saying 'Hey, forgot to tell you, there's a recall on the hardware.' Which, of course, he'd known all along because all the communication with the manufacturer went to his address. He just hadn't bothered to tell me."

"You don't still have the postcard, do you?" Jake asked.

"No. I didn't keep anything that would remind me of that creep." After sliding the lemon wedges into an overfull bowl, he covered it with plastic wrap. "I didn't kill him, but whoever did it has my sympathy. I ended up declaring bankruptcy, and people could have died."

A glance at Jake showed Penelope that he had no more questions, so she hopped off the barstool. "Thanks for your time."

"My pleasure. Come back and see the show. You'll have a good time."

"We will." Penelope beamed up at Jake and smiled wider as her husband sighed again.

THIRTEEN

Since it was still too early to expect the night manager to be at the Caribou Diner, Penelope did her evening rounds, giving Harold the cat his evening meal and insulin followed by the mandatory five minutes of chin scratching, giving grumpy Timmy the cat *his* evening meal and insulin with as little contact as possible, and offering Fluffy the Betta fish the amount of food that could be eaten in five minutes.

Then it was time to go to Esther's house, to feed the cats and sit with them for a while. But just as she turned the corner, Penelope saw her friend's wheelchair down the block, heading toward home at top speed.

Penelope jogged to meet her. "They let you go!"

Esther didn't slow. "The women's jail isn't ADA compliant. Vivica Hammer threatened to file a lawsuit, and suddenly that incompetent buffoon stopped pressuring Detective Sanchez to arrest me right away."

Penelope assumed the *incompetent buffoon* was Chief Purcell. It said something about Esther's state of mind that she'd used that language, because Esther worked hard to avoid dehumanizing anyone in speech, no matter what they'd done.

Another thought struck Penelope. "So... You have a get-out-of-jail-free card?"

Rolling up the ramp to her front door, Esther shook her head. "Penelope, I'm not going on a crime spree following whatever list you're about to write down."

"Okay, but maybe one or two tiny crimes?" Penelope waited for Esther to open the door, and followed her inside, where the cats raced around in excitement. "The world would be a better place afterward."

"I suspect he's holding off on arresting me until he finds out what it would cost to make the jail compliant."

After the cats had been fed and reassured that they were the most important beings in the universe, Penelope went to the back room to scoop litter boxes while Esther prepared her dinner.

"At least I found out why I'm in the running," Esther said, her voice carrying over the sound of three cats digging in the boxes Penelope was trying to clean.

"What's the reason?"

"The body was wrapped in the class welcome banner. Enough of it survived that they could tell it was from my class."

Penelope remembered the kindergarten welcome banner. Made from a plastic tablecloth, the banner had every student's name in large block letters. Normally it hung on the wall as a decoration, but it was pressed into service any time a tarp was needed or any class needed to block the light coming through a window.

Pirate dropped a mouse toy at Penelope's feet, so she tossed it across the room and he thundered after it. "What did you do with those at the end of the year?"

"Oh, I don't know. Most of them didn't last to the end of the year," Esther said. Something beeped, and she added more softly, "Yes, I know the door is open. Just give me a minute."

"Do you remember what happened *that* year?"

There was the distinctive squeak of the oven door hinges. "It could have been anything. One year, we used it to keep the roofing supplies stacked in the parking lot dry. Another year we had a chilly day and one of my kids forgot her jacket, so we made a poncho out of it and she wore it home."

Another appliance beeped, and she said, "You're all clamoring for attention like a pack of kids who've been sitting all day. Settle down." After a few more seconds, Esther continued, "Some years, the kids cut it apart so they could take the square with their name. And some years, whatever was left at the beginning of summer was thrown in the dumpster. I just don't remember what happened to it *that* year."

Penelope finally worked around the cats and finished with the litter boxes. She tossed Pirate's toy down the hallway and detoured into the bathroom to wash her hands, which immediately caused four cats to jump on the counter to watch the water come out of the faucet. "They won't be able to prove you were the only one to have access to it." She turned off the water and left the cats all trying to get in the sink.

If the banner was the only thing the police had against Esther, she wouldn't even need a high-powered lawyer like Hammerhead to be acquitted. The detectives had to have more.

Back in the kitchen, Penelope sat at the table and watched Esther make a béchamel sauce for the broccoli steaming in the microwave and told her everything she'd learned during the day. "Half the town hated him. They can't be focusing on you just because of the banner. Did they give you *any* other clues?"

Esther kept stirring. "I imagine it's because the police had an entire folder of complaints I'd filed against Brad and he'd filed against me. On paper, I'm the obvious suspect."

"Yes, but..."

Esther overrode Penelope's words. "And I might have done it, too, if I couldn't have come up with another way to keep that child safe."

Penelope grimaced. "Please tell me you didn't say that when you were being questioned."

Esther cackled. "Vivica would have slapped a hand across my mouth if I'd tried. That woman is a terror when she gets going."

"So I've heard." Penelope hadn't yet been arrested for anything serious enough to warrant spending the money on hiring Vivica Hammer, which should *not* have been a cause for disappointment.

Still, even if she didn't decide on a life of crime, there was no reason Penelope couldn't be falsely accused at some point in the future. In fact, with the way Chief Purcell felt about her, she probably had a decent chance of being declared enemy number one within the next year.

Penelope shook her head to clear those thoughts away. "It's probably whoever he was staying with after he left his wife. From all accounts, he was a horrible person."

Giving the sauce one last stir, Esther turned off the burner and maneuvered to face Penelope. "That's the thing. They seem to be under the assumption he died the night before the rosebush was planted."

That both made perfect sense and no sense at all. Penelope helped Frito climb onto her shoulders as she considered it. "As far as I can tell, nobody has admitted to seeing Brad after that night. But multiple people were getting postcards from him, at least until October. And he was *definitely* writing them — Rosella's lawyer had one tested for prints."

Steam billowed from the microwave when Esther opened the door. "I just don't see how anyone could have dug up the rosebush and replanted it six months later. The Rose Garden Society volunteers are there at least once a week."

Esther took the broccoli over to the stove as she continued. "Back then, Lewis Linderman was in charge of the cemetery crew and he noticed *everything*. Massimo backed over the Baron Girod de l'Ain near the entrance gate and tried to sneak in Commandant Beaurepaire, which nearly caused a riot when Lewis brought it up at the next meeting."

Penelope stared at her friend. Luckily, she hadn't yet come up with the words to ask why Massimo running over some poor man had anything to do with the Rose Garden Society when Esther continued.

"Though of course, that Baron Girod de l'Ain really didn't like the location — the aphids covered it, which was a sign it wasn't healthy in the first place — and we were on the verge of admitting defeat anyhow, and the Commandant Beaurepaire has thrived so well in the same spot that it's almost a nuisance, and if we didn't prune it severely, it would scratch everyone coming through the gate."

Penelope closed her mouth and tried to look as if she'd always known Baron Girod de l'Ain and Commandant Beaurepaire were special plants. Apparently, there was a veritable army of rosebushes in the cemetery. She wrenched her thoughts back to the important part of the conversation.

"Maybe someone dug a tunnel and put the body there without digging up the rosebush first?"

"In that soil? Not a chance."

Penelope remembered the rock-hard clay in the areas Matteo hadn't soaked. Esther was right. No modern version of *The Great Escape* would have let anyone place Brad Squires's body under that rosebush from afar. "Obviously, the only answer is that Brad was killed and buried and his ghost wrote a bunch of postcards over the next six months."

Esther didn't dignify that with a response. "Would you like to stay for dinner? I have enough for two."

Penelope stood and lifted Frito from her shoulders. "Thanks, but Jake and I are going to the Caribou Diner tonight to talk to Big Wayne. I have to leave room for the Mighty Moose combo."

Esther shook her head. "Oh, to be young."

Penelope laughed. "I'll stop by in the morning and let you know how it went." She was still grinning as she let herself through the door without allowing the cats to dart out, but that smile turned to a frown as she walked home in the darkening streets, wondering how a man could be buried six months before he died.

FOURTEEN

The Caribou Diner had been built during a time when distinctive architecture was expected and celebrated. Later builders had put together buildings more economically, and most of those were cheaper to maintain and keep comfortable, but the Caribou Diner had panache.

Rust leaked from beneath the metal sheets covering the two giant antlers attached to the rounded arch of the entry-way, and the left antler tilted in a way that suggested it might be shed in the next storm. But the parking lot was never empty and people drove from fifty miles away to spend a few hours drinking endless black coffee in a relaxed and casual atmosphere.

Inside, the diner looked as it always had, with plush vinyl booths and Formica tables. Booster seats and high-chairs were available, and Big Wayne had been known to entertain children with drawing lessons in an adjoining booth to allow weary parents to eat in peace. Big Wayne himself was a huge bald man who had to duck to go through doorways. His arms were completely covered in tattoos of anime characters in front of a backdrop of high-rises. The tattoos disappeared into the sleeves of the green Caribou Diner t-shirt that stretched across his barrel chest, and Penelope had always assumed most of his body was covered in ink, though she'd never had a good reason to find out.

Since it wasn't yet midnight, there was still a cook and server, but Big Wayne jumped up from the booth next to the door when Penelope and Jake walked in. "Welcome to the Caribou Diner! Great to see you again!" He gestured toward the empty booths on the left. "Pick a seat. I'll take your order whenever you're ready."

"Two Mighty Moose combos," Penelope said promptly. "One without green onions and one with green onions and jalapeños. Orange soda for me and..." She looked at Jake.

"Decaf coffee," he said. "And if you have a convenient moment, we'd like to talk to you."

Big Wayne raised his eyebrows and looked down at them. "This about Brad Squires?"

Penelope nodded. "The police chief is working to pin the murder on a friend of ours, so we're trying to get a better idea of what Brad was like." Halfway through the sentence, she realized it sounded like they were talking to people in order to find other suspects — which wasn't completely inaccurate — but Big Wayne merely nodded.

"It might be a few minutes since Amber's on her break. Have a seat and I'll put your orders in and get your drinks."

Penelope picked the booth next to the window and smiled when Jake slid in next to her. "Have enough room?"

He stretched both arms up and then rested one on her shoulder. "Wouldn't want Big Wayne to feel crowded."

"You're so compassionate." Penelope snuggled closer to him. "It's one of the things I love about you."

"Hm." His arm tightened around her. "I may have also had an ulterior motive."

Penelope smiled into his shoulder. "That's another thing I love about you."

"Honesty is important in any relationship," he said gravely. "Speaking of which, did Brutus *really* get onto the counter to eat that soufflé Brian made, or did you leave it in his dish?"

Penelope paused for a moment as she tried to figure out the best way to word her answer. "I... might have tripped and dropped it on the ground. It was so rubbery. And Brian was so proud of it that we would have had to eat it every day until it was gone."

Jake kissed the top of her head. "And that's what I love about you."

Big Wayne dropped off their drinks, but didn't stay, as a woman at another table was looking around in the universal sign she needed something.

Penelope sipped her orange soda, a favorite from her childhood and something she only drank these days at the Caribou Diner. "Did you get a copy of the Wags Forever contract?"

"Yes. It's interesting reading. What did you want to know?"

Of course Jake had not only obtained the contract but had actually read it through. Penelope wasn't surprised. "Do they promise to house the animal until they die? Is that explicitly stated?"

"Yes." He sipped his coffee. "Isn't that the point?"

"Depends on the rescue. Brutus — for a completely random example — would do better in someone's home. Some rescues accept bequests on the understanding that the pet will be taken care of, which may mean the rescue has an adoption center and pays for expenses after the animal is adopted. If Wags Forever is adopting dogs out, that would explain why they don't have many animals staying there." She thought back to the facility they'd visited. "Though I'd expect them to publicize the location a little more if they were trying to draw in potential adopters."

He shook his head. "No, they promise to keep the pet there until a veterinarian and the rescue director agree that the pet's quality of life is too poor to continue. There's an entire section of the contract that spells everything out." He set his coffee back on the saucer. "I'm comfortable advising Esther and her friend that Wags Forever is a bad choice. I'll start looking into the others tomorrow."

Esther had hired Jake to find out if her friend with the horrible rat terriers was making a good decision in relying on Wags Forever. They now had an answer to that, so the case would technically be finished as soon as Jake checked into the other two rescues. But if there was something shady happening at Wags Forever, Penelope wanted to shut it down before more people signed over their life savings. "After we get Esther in the clear from this murder, I want to come back to this."

"I've already penciled it in on the schedule," Jake assured her. "Right after finding Brian a place to live."

"Also very important," Penelope agreed. "And we're hosting the book group next week, so I need to spend a few hours vacuuming the crumbs from the couch. And maybe shampooing the living room carpet, if you'll let me borrow your gadget." Jake had recently purchased a carpet steam cleaner. His justification was that Brutus drooled so much that vacuuming the floor wasn't enough. That was definitely true, but Penelope thought he just enjoyed watching the sudsy water being sucked back into the machine.

"Hands off my gadget. I'll do it. Didn't we just host it a few months ago?"

"We did, but June's sister-in-law is visiting and she — the sister-in-law — is a militant teetotaler. June's words, not mine. But since the point of book club is to sit around drinking wine..."

Jake turned to look at her. "You know, if you'd mentioned that when you invited me, I might have joined."

Penelope held up her index finger. "I believe your exact words were, 'I think I'm busy that night.' And since I never had a chance to tell you *when* it was, I never had a chance to tell you about the wine. But if you still want in, you're welcome to stay. June has good taste in wines. And cheese."

"And the book?"

"It's not bad. You might even like this one. It's a thriller and the main character is an accountant." In the same way that Penelope couldn't read stories with dogs where it was clear the author had never owned a pet, Jake refused to read or watch anything with characters on the police force. It made finding something to read or watch together difficult.

"I'll consider it."

Before Penelope could encourage Jake further, Big Wayne slid into the booth across from them and set down a coffee pot with a bright orange rim. "Amber's boyfriend broke up with her while she was on her break, so she's gone home and I'll be running around for a bit. What did you need to ask me?"

"Tell us about Brad," Penelope answered promptly. Jake preferred uninterrupted interviews, but that had been easier to accomplish when he was the acting chief of police. In contrast, Penelope didn't mind asking questions in a scattered manner. It gave her time to filter out all the random thoughts floating through her brain, from new treats to try on stubborn dogs, to whether she could write off peanut butter on her taxes, and get back to the topic at hand.

Crossing his arms on the table in front of him, Big Wayne grimaced and stared at the Formica. "Not firing him the first time someone complained is my biggest regret in life." The tattoo of a spiky-haired boy on a motorcycle jumped as he tensed his arms. "I learned an important lesson: some people are masters of acting one way to their boss and like a completely different person to someone who can't cause problems."

Penelope wondered if he'd done the artwork for his own tattoos. They certainly looked like the drawings she'd seen. She stored that question away to ask later. "What was the complaint about?"

"One of the front desk staff had questioned some numbers Brad had given her for the brochure she was putting together. She told me he got in her space and she felt unsafe." He shook his head, still looking at the table. "I should have trusted her instincts. My only excuse was that I was younger, and I'd been promoted to a management job with zero training. But still. I screwed up."

Then he smiled and met Penelope's eyes. "The woman who complained has my old job now and she's amazing at it. I send these kids over to work for her if they want to move out of food service." The bell over the door jangled. "I'll be back."

After Big Wayne had left to seat a trio of men, Penelope looked over at her husband. "That fits with everything else we know about Brad. He intimidated anyone he thought he could control and managed to hide that side from everyone else."

"Or at least not give them any evidence," Jake agreed. "Brian knew. My guess is that all the patrol officers knew and were just waiting for him to mess up so they could document what they could." He shifted in his seat. "We should get the name of the woman who complained."

"You think she'll tell us anything we don't know?"

"Probably not. But I think standing up to someone like Brad Squires potentially put her in danger. Guys like that don't like to be crossed, especially by women, and even more especially by women in jobs they see as beneath them. If Brad was planning to leave town, he might have considered settling old scores. A woman who'd had her complaints dismissed once before might not want to risk arguing she was acting in self-defense."

Penelope watched a toddler three tables away tear apart a piece of toast. "A more suspicious person might note that Big Wayne pointed us at another suspect, but I'll give him the benefit of the doubt here. He seems truly sorry he didn't handle the situation better." Penelope frowned. "Normally I'm glad there's no statute of limitation for murder, but in this case... Whoever killed Brad Squires might have made the world a better place."

Jake grunted in agreement.

After a ding from the kitchen, Big Wayne was back with their food. "Let me get this other order in and I'll be back," he promised.

True to his word, he returned right as Penelope ate the last jalapeño slice and offered her remaining cheese-drenched fries to her husband. "Everything okay here?" He sat down again. "I have a few minutes before table three is going to want their check. More questions?"

This time, Jake took the lead. "Tell us about the audit."

Big Wayne blew out a short breath. "I got a call from the bank on a Friday afternoon saying we didn't have enough to cover a check we'd sent to a vendor. There had been a mix-up earlier that month with all the summer program payments being deposited in the wrong account, and I thought we were still dealing with the fallout from that. The bank covered the check with money from a different account and we all left for the weekend."

Penelope winced. She'd heard enough embezzlement stories to know what happened next. Big Wayne caught the movement and nodded. "Yeah. On Monday, I asked around to find out how to have an audit done." He huffed a laugh. "That should tell you how poorly prepared I was for that job."

During the many jobs she'd held, Penelope had seen plenty of people unprepared for their current role, often with disastrous results. "You were doing your best."

"I was. And at that point, I still thought the money was just in the wrong place and we only needed some help to straighten things out. But of course Brad must have heard me calling people — his desk was right outside my office. He didn't show up the next day and I still didn't get it. It wasn't until the auditor called me up an hour after I handed over the accounts that I knew anything was really wrong."

Jake methodically wiped cheese from his fingers. "How much did he end up with?"

"I think the final total was just above thirty thousand."

There was a moment of silence at the table as Jake and Penelope digested that information. That wouldn't be enough to live off forever, but if Brad had planned to leave, it would have made a nice relocation bonus.

Jake recovered first. "How much did they recover?"

"None, as far as I know. Some he'd been transferring to his own accounts and cashing out as soon as it went in. And he'd also been pocketing the cash deposits and transferring funds from other accounts to confuse things. He had to know it was all going to come crashing down at some point, but I guess he was just trying to see how much he could get before he disappeared."

Big Wayne looked around the diner fondly. "You know, though...Things worked out for me in the end. After I was fired, this was the only place that would hire me. Started as a busboy and worked my way up. And I learned my lesson. I handle the deposits for my shift, and if anyone ever tells me they feel unsafe, I handle it right away."

He stood and went to table three to give them their bill.

Jake waited until Big Wayne was out of earshot before speaking. "So on Monday night, Brad Squires potentially had tens of thousands of dollars in cash with him when he disappeared."

Penelope used her knife to draw a winged pig in the congealing cheese sauce. "Detective Sanchez would have mentioned if they'd found a bag of cash with the body, right?"

"Almost certainly." Jake didn't need to add that Brianna wouldn't have told *Penelope*, but she would have said something to Jake.

Setting her knife down, Penelope sighed. "I think the police might be right."

Jake looked at her plate. "Ah. That explains your artwork."

"I think Brad died sometime Monday night." Never mind for the moment that somehow postcards with his handwriting and fingerprints showed up for the next six months. "Even ignoring the rosebush, there's no way a young man with a stack of cash would remain unseen for six months. You or I might manage it..." She stopped when Jake made a noise between coughing and choking.

Jake had a point. One time Penelope had been taking antibiotics that caused sun sensitivity, and her plan to spend the next ten days indoors had quickly changed to using an umbrella for shade during the daytime. Keeping out of sight for any length of time was not on her list of abilities.

"Okay, fine, *you* might manage to stay out of sight for six months if you had the right motivation, but nothing we've heard about Brad even hints he could do it."

"Agreed," Jake said, using his spoon to give the pig a background of clouds. "Even if he'd been holed up at a friend's place, somebody would have talked."

"Did he have any friends?" Penelope considered all the conversations she'd had about Brad. "Even his brother said he rubbed people the wrong way. And if you can't get your family to say nice things about you..."

"It means we have a bigger problem, though."

"Never let it be said that I can't take a big problem and make it worse," Penelope said with a smile. "But how?"

"Well, not us, necessarily, but whoever has to put the case together," Jake amended. "We've been looking for someone who had a motive to kill Brad."

Penelope nodded. "Of which there are quite a few for someone so young. I always assumed it took a lifetime of bad deeds to give that many people a motive. Even *I* don't have that many people poking pins in a voodoo doll dressed like me, and I'm twice the age he was when he died."

Jake's lips twitched. "Don't sell yourself short. I've seen what happens when you go to the Rose Garden Society meetings."

Penelope opened her mouth to defend herself and then closed it again. She refused to let him draw her into a discussion of the Winter Fair decorations meeting again.

After a pause to give her time to speak, Jake leaned over to kiss her cheek. "You were absolutely justified in what you said and I stand behind you one hundred percent."

"Because I was right." She gave the pig a unicorn horn. "Back to Brad. You said we had been looking for someone with a motive to kill him, and I said there was a list."

"Yes. But if he was carrying all that money on him, it didn't have to be someone with a grudge. Someone might have killed him for the cash."

The sinking feeling in Penelope's stomach wasn't from too many Mighty Moose Fries. Clearing Esther's name by solving a twenty-five-year-old murder would be hard enough if they had some idea of who wanted Brad Squires dead.

If the killer could be anyone at all, solving the case might be impossible.

FIFTEEN

The dark house was silent as Penelope crept downstairs.

Or... it would have been silent if Brutus hadn't been following her. Between his collar tags jingling with each step, his wagging tail hitting the wall twice per second, and his full weight hitting each step as he danced in excitement, it was a little like traveling with her own personal one-man band. But everyone who stayed more than one night in the house learned how to tune out Brutus as he alternately patrolled the house and picked different spots to sleep and snore loudly.

Normally, Penelope fell asleep the minute her head touched the pillow, worn out by the activities of the day. But after an hour of staring at the ceiling and making pictures from the shadows and wondering why she was still awake, she had finally remembered that the brand of orange soda served at the Caribou Diner contained caffeine. In her youth, caffeine hadn't affected her sleep patterns, but lately she'd noticed that was no longer true.

Faced with another hour or two of staring at the ceiling

or getting up and doing something, she chose the latter, carefully sliding out of bed so she didn't wake Jake, who had sensibly *not* ingested caffeine right before bedtime.

The guest room door was closed, so Penelope sat on the couch with her laptop, placing a cushion behind her where Jake normally sat. Brutus heaved himself onto the end of the couch and sat on her feet. She patted his flank. "Thanks for keeping my feet warm." Brutus snorted in reply and two seconds later, his snores filled the room.

Was it morbid to have a folder of photographs dedicated to Brad Squires's murder? Penelope flipped through them, seeing the muddy grave with the doomed rosebush still standing, and Rosella's forwarded pictures of the postcards, taken to document the threats Brad had made.

Except Brad had already been dead by then.

Pulling up a spreadsheet, she added a row for every postcard she'd heard about, color coding them by their level of threat. Some were seemingly innocuous, comments on Rosella's recent haircut or dress. Penelope colored those rows yellow.

Orange rows were gleefully malicious, such as the postcard notifying Vincent Collins of the fireplace insert recall received after a house nearly burned down. Esther had remembered a couple of those as well: a card noting that she'd been trapped in her house after a large storm had dropped a tree limb on the ramp to her front door, and a scrawled condolence on a cat's death with a smiley face at the bottom.

The odd thing about the latter was that the cat's death had been entirely natural and expected, a result of age-related kidney failure. In fact, without the smiley face and Brad's signature, Esther would have assumed it had been meant kindly. Sandwich had been found at school as a kitten, Esther had taken him home to raise, and fifteen years of kindergarten classes had known him through a photo collage on the wall. The local paper had even run two stories about him — one when it heard he was sick, and another after the cat had passed away a year later.

Red was reserved for postcards that had been outright threats, such as Brad's complaint about his son's court jester Halloween costume.

Her contemplation of the spreadsheet was interrupted by Jake coming down the stairs. Brutus jumped off the couch to escort him, and Penelope took the opportunity to stretch her toes. "The antacids are on the counter," she told her husband in a low voice. Jake may have chosen decaf coffee, but a burger and cheese-slathered fries that late in the evening would have triggered his acid reflux.

"How am I supposed to complain if you tell me how to fix it first?" he grumbled, voice rough from sleep. He went into the kitchen and there was the sound of chewable tablets falling against the side of the plastic container. Then the sound of water running, which *almost* masked the sound of the dog treat bag opening.

Penelope waited until her husband came into the living room with a glass of water. "When your dog wakes you up in the middle of the night because he expects treats, I'll have no sympathy." She sat up so he could move the cushions and take his place at the end of the couch behind her, while Brutus returned to his spot on her feet.

"*Our* dog would never do such a thing," Jake declared. "I hope your spreadsheet has nothing to do with our finances. Lots of warning colors there."

"I think I've figured out *how* the postcards were sent when Brad was dead and buried under a prize rosebush, but I still have no idea *why*."

"Presumably to disguise the fact that he was dead," Jake offered. "As long as everyone thought Brad was alive, nobody was thinking about the possibility he'd been killed."

"Right, but..." Penelope scrolled up to the top of her spreadsheet. "Back up a little. I wish we had the originals to be sure, but I think most of the postcards were the equivalent of me knowing you had a stomachache before you said anything. That was not a meal people in their fifties should have late at night."

"You're saying my stomach is *not* the result of you shoving pins into a voodoo doll?"

"Heavens, no. I have your doll deep cleaning the kitchen. I'd never stick pins in it." She felt the rumble of his laugh behind her. "I know you. And if I didn't have to say exactly *when* it would happen in the next six months, I could accurately predict that you would have a stomachache due to eating something late at night."

Jake's sigh tickled the back of her neck. "As much as I'd like to think I'm still capable of change, you're probably right."

"But you see my point, right? I'm a little surprised he paid enough attention to the people around him to come up with everything, but Brad *could* have written all those postcards before he died in April — as long as someone *else* was responsible for sending them out at the right time."

Jake reached past her to increase the font size and then was silent for nearly a full minute as he read what she'd written. "I see what you mean. But that brings up *two* questions."

"Why would Brad write all those postcards in advance," Penelope supplied, "and...?"

"Who was his accomplice?" Jake answered.

Penelope leaned forward so she could twist to look at her husband. "Accomplice? You mean murderer."

"Not necessarily." Jake waited until Penelope had extricated her feet from under the dog so she could sit next to him more comfortably. "What was the point of having all the postcards written out in advance?"

"To keep anyone from noticing Brad was decomposing in the cemetery," Penelope answered promptly.

"Yes, that was the result, but back up a bit. From Brad's point of view — assuming he hadn't intended to get murdered — what were the postcards supposed to accomplish?"

Penelope closed the laptop and placed it on the coffee table so she didn't have to worry about it sliding onto the floor. Naturally, Brutus took that as a sign that she'd cleared space for him and flopped around until his head weighed down her lap. She absently rubbed his ear as she thought about what Jake had asked. "It kept Rosella and Esther worried about him."

Jake nodded. "But I think that may have just been a bonus for him. What else?"

"It made everyone think he was still somewhere in town." Understanding dawned. "Including the cops."

"Exactly. He knew it wouldn't be long before the embezzlement was noticed — Big Wayne was already talking about an audit. And it was the city's money, so the police would definitely be involved. But the department's resources are limited. And if everyone is convinced Brad is still in town..."

Penelope nodded as she thought about that. "He could have been lying on a sunny beach in Mexico with the trail getting colder every day." She ran one finger down the groove between Brutus's eyes and the dog groaned in delight. "It's not a bad plan. I mean, aside from him being an abusive jerk who wanted to terrorize people after he was gone."

"Aside from that," Jake agreed. "But it only works if he has an accomplice in town, someone who can pick the perfect time to send the postcards."

"Right."

The room was silent as they both considered that, until Brutus resumed snoring. Finally, Penelope said, "Who would do that, though? I get helping a friend out. If Esther needed to flee the country, I'd be the first to help confuse her trail."

Jake rubbed his face with one hand and stayed silent.

Penelope continued. "But I wouldn't help her terrorize anyone. Not that Esther would do that." She paused. "Esther might tell a few truths people didn't want to hear, but that's different. She would never make anyone feel unsafe."

Jake reached over to pet Brutus. "It's interesting that Esther is the one you're going to help flee the country and not, say, your husband."

Penelope looked at him, startled. "Well, I couldn't very well send postcards for you since I'd be going along."

A slow smile creased Jake's face, making Penelope's toes tingle. Or possibly that was from the weight of Brutus's head on her lap. She reminded herself that Brian was asleep on the other side of the guest bedroom door. "But my point was, his accomplice wasn't a very nice person. They probably wouldn't think twice about murder."

Jake tipped his head forward to rest against hers. "If I agree with you, will you come back to bed?"

"Only if you can find something for me to do until all the caffeine wears off." Penelope attempted an innocent look, though from the way Jake was suppressing a smile, she'd missed the mark.

Jake nodded. "I'm sure I can think of something."

"And you might have to carry me." Penelope tried to move out from under the dog. "I think my legs have fallen asleep."

SIXTEEN

The benefit of living and working in a relatively small town was the ability to learn something about everyone. As a pet sitter and part-time mail carrier, Penelope had access to a lot of information. Plus, all that time she spent outside gave her a chance to observe people.

Though sometimes tempted, Penelope tried to only use that knowledge for good. Normally, she wouldn't dream of ambushing Dr. Marsh outside of her veterinary practice. Or inside her practice, for that matter. But even if Penelope came up with a reason for Brutus to need an appointment, it would take weeks to get in. And she wasn't sure this was the sort of thing Celia Marsh would want to discuss where clients and coworkers might overhear.

So at six-thirty the next morning, Penelope stationed herself at a table inside Brewster's Coffee, a small shop on the edge of the park where Celia Marsh jogged every weekday morning. Brewster's was renowned for indifferent service and the owner's battle against lingering customers. There were no personal greetings for regulars or free wifi at Brewsters, and anything after the first two modifications to a cup of coffee was ignored. For a while, Penelope had wondered if the shop was a money laundering operation, but after going a few times, she'd decided it was a refreshing antidote to the big chains with their forced smiles and upsells. Sometimes it was nice to be at a place where nobody knew your name, or at least pretended not to.

At this time of day, there were too many people in line for Leo to accost anyone taking longer than fifteen minutes to drink their beverage and leave, but Penelope still planned to get up and buy a pastry if Dr. Marsh didn't appear before her coffee was cold.

The door swung open to admit a man speaking into his phone. "No, that won't work for us. You tell Virgil he needs to go back to Moorhouse and demand the..." He continued in jargon so technical that Penelope couldn't even tell what industry he was in, though she had sympathy for both the person on the other end of the call and also Virgil, whoever he was. The man got to the front of the line, still talking on the phone, and, without pausing, told the cashier with vivid blue hair, "Venti cold brew latte half-oat, half-soy, three pumps raspberry, two pumps caramel."

He waved his credit card over the reader impatiently, even as he turned sideways and continued the conversation on the phone. "... and don't let him tell you he can't do that before Tuesday, because he's got all weekend." He paused and looked at the cashier, because the credit card reader still hadn't beeped.

She pointed to the large sign in front of the register. *Please no cell phone use at counter.* "We don't —"

He rolled his eyes and talked over her. "Venti cold brew latte half-oat, half-soy, three pumps raspberry, two pumps caramel." Then he turned sideways. "This is ridiculous. Where was I? Oh yeah, don't let him tell you he can't get to it before Tuesday. If he wants to stay in business, he needs to..."

By this time, everyone in the coffee shop had turned to watch the show. Penelope had only been to Brewster's Coffee a few times, but even she knew what happened next. The barista with the blue hair moved to the side to work on orders, and Leo stepped up behind the register.

Leo was over six feet and built like a champion weightlifter, though his wrinkled ears suggested he'd spent his youth in boxing gyms. One time Penelope had overheard him discussing eighteenth-century French philosophers with the blue-haired barista. But with difficult customers, he leaned on his looks and reputation.

Now he loomed over the counter and stared into the other man's eyes. "No cell phones. You can have plain coffee or you can go away."

The man rocked back. "But... That's not what I want."

Leo shrugged. "Then you can go away. All you get today is plain coffee. Other drinks are for people who can read signs and be polite." He raised his eyebrows and waited.

To Penelope's surprise, the man said meekly, "I'll have the coffee."

Leo leaned back to his side of the counter and smiled pleasantly. "Good choice."

Penelope was so caught up in the drama that she didn't notice Dr. Marsh in line two people behind Cell Phone Guy until she heard the veterinarian's familiar voice ordering a large flat white to go. It was what she ordered every workday after her run, and she drank it during her cool down walk around the park.

Jumping to her feet, Penelope followed the veterinarian out of the coffee shop. "Dr. Marsh, do you mind if I walk with you? I need to talk to you about something."

The veterinarian's neutral expression froze, but Penelope would have missed it if she hadn't been expecting it. She kept walking. "I can't give medical advice without examining your pet." Then she turned her head to look at Penelope. "You're Brutus's owner, right? Ms. ... Standing? If you call the hospital during regular office hours, we should be able to fit him in."

"Penelope," she confirmed, pleased that she'd been remembered. "But this isn't for Brutus. Or even one of my pet sitting clients." Before Dr. Marsh could make another assumption, she added, "This is about Wags Forever."

"Oh." After another five steps, Dr. Marsh said, "I can't disclose any information about other people's pets."

That pause felt significant, as if Dr. Marsh had things to say, if only she wasn't constrained by confidentiality. Penelope's heart rate increased — she was definitely on to something.

The sidewalk going away from the coffee shop split into a concrete walkway to the street and an unpaved path that looped around the park. Both women turned left to walk on the sandy path. In the field with soccer goals set up at either end, a man threw a tennis ball for a German shorthair pointer, but there was nobody within earshot.

"I know you can't tell me anything," Penelope started. "But my husband — he's a private detective now — was hired to look into Wags Forever, to see if it was the right place for a client to send her dogs when she can no longer care for them."

"Ah." Dr. Marsh took a sip of her coffee without slowing. "I can email you a list of rescue group recommendations when I get to the office."

If Penelope had been considering donating money to Wags Forever, that response would have been enough for her to change her plans. It also gave her hope that Dr. Marsh wanted to address this problem as much as she could without crossing legal or ethical lines.

Penelope jumped over a puddle left by overzealous sprinkler use, careful not to slosh her coffee all over her hand. "That would be helpful. My husband and I took a tour of the facility this week, and I noticed that quite a few of the dogs looked familiar." She glanced at Dr. Marsh. "With all the pet sitting I do, I spend a lot of time at the dog park and meeting dogs on walks." She frowned. "Some days I wish I was a little better at remembering people's names, but I usually only remember the dog's name."

"It's a challenge," Dr. Marsh agreed. "I had to start using memory tricks to remember the name of the person attached to each pet." She continued before Penelope could ask. "Brutus is standing on a penny and is holding a big wheel with 'Jake' stamped on the rim in his mouth. That's enough to remind me."

"Penelope Standing and Jake Wheeler," Penelope said, delighted with this trick. "That's amazing!"

"The more ridiculous the image, the easier it is to remember."

Penelope considered this as she watched a white SUV slow, as if the driver was going to park, and then speed up again, apparently deciding on a spot closer to their goal. It always amazed her how many people drove two blocks to the park so they could fight over the three marked spaces closest to the entrance path, when they could approach the park from any direction and walk across ten feet of grass to end up on the same path.

Dr. Marsh took a sip of her coffee. "You were saying that you recognized the dogs there..."

Pulling her thoughts back from memory tricks and the

strange ways people lived their lives, Penelope focussed on the reason she'd waylaid the veterinarian. "When we took the tour, the woman in charge..." She paused, trying to remember her name.

Dr. Marsh suggested, "Jessica Green?" When Penelope nodded gratefully, she said, "I picture her wearing a green jester's costume."

After a confused moment, Penelope realized that was the image the veterinarian used to remember the woman's name. "That's genius. But yes, Jessica showed us around and implied that the dogs at the facility had been taken in as part of the rescue. But I recognized most of those dogs and they have homes. Maybe they're also running a doggy day care, but even if they are, where are all the dogs that are supposed to be at the rescue?"

If they *were* running a doggy day care, she thought they would have to have a business license. And a lot of insurance, if they were smart. She'd have to mention that to Jake when she next saw him — he was good at tracking down that sort of thing.

Dr. Marsh seemed to be choosing her words carefully. "I'm not sure there's anything I can tell you about that other than Wags Forever is no longer a client of the practice."

So the rescue had done something that made Dr. Marsh sever ties with them. It might have been something as simple as not paying their bills on time, but Penelope thought there was more to it. Unfortunately, Dr. Marsh would still be bound by confidentiality rules, even if something else had happened.

What Penelope needed was a list of dogs that should have been at the rescue, but without breaking into the facility and going through their files — an option Jake would definitely frown upon, though she wasn't completely ruling it out — she didn't see a way to get one. But Dr. Marsh would have such a list, or at least, she knew which animals she'd seen at the facility and unless they had died, they should still be there.

"Jessica said you are the veterinarian they use. And I know you can't tell me anything about their medical history, but someone needs to track the dogs that people have sent to the rescue. If they aren't there, where are they?"

For nearly a minute, the only sound was their shoes crunching on the sandy path. Finally, Penelope said, "If an anonymous source sent a list of the dogs that *should* be there, we could start looking for them. If they've been re-homed, which the contract doesn't allow, and we find them, we can go back to the original owner or their family." She waited a moment and then decided she'd done her best to convince the other woman. "Let me give you my card. My email address is on there."

For a moment, she thought Dr. Marsh wouldn't take it from her. Then the veterinarian plucked the rectangle from Penelope's hand and shoved it in the pocket of her shorts. "No promises."

"None needed. Maybe we'll figure out some other way to audit their books. But I think if they promise to keep a dog for the rest of its life, they should stand by their word." After another few strides, Penelope decided she should leave before she said something to ruin any good will she had left. "Thanks for listening. Sorry again for tracking you down outside of work."

"I understand." She gave Penelope a weary smile. "Just... please don't make a habit of it."

Penelope cut across the grass toward her next pet sitting job and left Dr. Marsh to finish her loop around the park.

SEVENTEEN

Esther was in good spirits when Penelope stopped by before lunch to clip all the cats' nails. The police had not called her back in for questioning, her sourdough starter was ready to be split up and distributed to the baking network, and the rose grafts on the porch looked promising.

"If everything goes well, we can have that section of the cemetery back to normal in a couple of years." The entire room had the comforting yeasty smell of unbaked bread, partially because there was a loaf of bread rising on the counter, but also from the seven jars partially filled with Jane Dough.

"Until they have to dig half of it up to find Elmer so they can ship his dirt off to another cemetery." Penelope repositioned Barnaby in her lap so she could get to his front legs. The tuxedo didn't mind nail trims, but he liked to lounge in odd positions that made it hard to see what she was doing.

Esther finished writing on another tag, threaded ribbon through the hole, and looped it around a glass jar a quarter full of bubbly sourdough starter. "No. Didn't you hear?

Derek and Matteo found the right plot yesterday. They've boxed up the remains and sent them on their way."

Penelope clipped one more nail and looked up. "That seems..." She paused, searching for the right word.

"Miraculous?" Esther supplied.

Barnaby rolled onto his back on Penelope's lap and she took advantage of the new position to work on his other paw. "I'm not sure I would bring a deity into this. I was thinking more... unlikely."

Esther slid a blank tag from the pile. "It was definitely *convenient* to dig another hole in the ground and find Elmer's remains while there were no witnesses."

It was certainly the solution Penelope would have chosen if *she'd* been in charge. "At least this way, Derek doesn't have to tell the public that half the headstones are over the wrong graves."

"Oh, it's not anywhere close to half."

"How do you know?" Penelope bounced the cat on her lap to distract him while she clipped the most difficult nail, the right thumb. "You told me that nobody knows for sure how many people Massimo put in the wrong place." She finished and gave Barnaby a treat and a snuggle before setting him on the floor and tossing the ball.

"Because when the headstones were placed, most families remembered roughly where the burial had been. If there was a discrepancy, they would talk to Massimo and he would move the headstone when Thea wasn't around." Esther paused in threading ribbon through another card. "Of course, there were some mix-ups during the headstone restorations about twenty years ago. Some of the older graves may not be entirely correct."

Penelope laughed softly as she wandered around the living room, searching for Frito. "And yet somehow Matteo and Derek magically located Elmer's remains on the second try." She lifted the fluffy white Persian from the top of the cat tree. "Probably afraid they were going to find more murder victims if they dug too many holes."

At the kitchen table, Esther began screwing lids on jars. "There can't be *that* many bodies. We haven't had that many missing persons."

Penelope sat at the table again, keeping a hand on Frito to keep the cat from climbing onto her shoulders. "Sure, but Brad Squires wasn't a missing person, either. So who knows? There could be more." Her phone rang, and she answered it before Esther could reply. "Hi, Jake."

Her husband's voice was level and quiet, a sure sign that something was going on and he didn't want anyone around him to overhear their conversation. "We have a situation at home."

"That doesn't sound promising."

"Purcell showed up with a search warrant about an hour ago."

Penelope stared at her phone in disbelief. In the back of her mind, she cataloged the things she'd done that *might* cause a search warrant to be issued, but she'd certainly never stored anything incriminating in the house she and Jake shared. "What is he looking for?"

"The gun used to kill Brad Squires." In the background, there was a shout of triumph. "And I think he just found it."

EIGHTEEN

When Penelope arrived home, slightly breathless from sprinting the entire way, Jake met her on the driveway. There was one patrol unit and another unmarked car at the curb in addition to Brian's motorcycle, but her husband was the only person outside. She'd intended to go straight into the house, but Jake gathered her into his arms and whispered, "If you get arrested for punching the chief of police, that would make me responsible for getting insulin into Timmy tonight."

"Ugh." Penelope made a face and relaxed against him. "I hate it when you're right." It would have been so cathartic to confront Purcell, but Jake had a point. Purcell had the power to dump her in a jail cell for a day or two, even if charges were never filed.

That would let down everyone who depended on her, including Timmy, the diabetic cat who could be incredibly unpredictable. Some days he purred and rubbed his cheeks all over everybody walking through the front door; other days, he snarled and hissed. His previous pet sitter had quit after being pinned in the bathroom and having to escape through the window. Penelope had learned to read the subtle twitch of Timmy's ears that meant she shouldn't touch him for at least ten minutes, but that was a hard skill to teach.

Taking a deep breath, Penelope set her shoulders and stood up straight so she could look at her husband's face. "Okay, I'm ready to listen now. Why would they get a warrant to search *our* place for the gun used to shoot someone neither of us knew, and where did they find the thing?"

"Anonymous tip." One eyebrow quirked up, which told her what he thought about *that*. "And they found it up in the rafters in the garage."

"With the cursed soap?" They had put the mottled orange soap Penelope had made in the rafters to cure, but neither had brought up taking it down to use or give away. Though Jake had once remarked that they hadn't had a rodent problem in the garage for a while. In the meantime, the odor had faded, so the garage merely had a pleasant floral scent instead of the original olfactory assault — mostly because Jake kept the garage door open whenever possible.

"From what I heard, right in the middle of it."

Penelope winced. "Does metal pick up odors?"

"If it does, they may have to close the evidence room."

Chief Purcell and Detective Sanchez stood near the front door, discussing something in low tones. Or rather, Purcell was listening with an increasingly red face as Brianna urgently spoke, occasionally looking over at Penelope.

Penelope frowned. "Purcell can't honestly think I've been hiding the murder weapon for twenty-five years. I moved fifteen times and had all my possessions in two clear plastic storage tubs for most of it. And you only bought this house a few years ago."

"I *think* the idea is that you are supposed to have taken it from Esther when it became clear that her house would be searched."

Penelope took half a step back, offended. "Why is everyone assuming it was me? I'd hardly hide a gun in the garage. That's *your* area."

The corner of Jake's mouth rose. "I see you're not even going to attempt to convince me you wouldn't have done the crime, just that you wouldn't have done it like *that*."

"Well, it's Esther." Which was all the explanation Penelope needed to give. If Esther had asked her to do something like that, she would have had an excellent reason. "Anyhow, *I* would have hidden it somewhere else where Brutus couldn't get to it, like at the bottom of his food bin or in the back of the freezer. Or chucked it up into a tree in the park." She thought about that idea for a moment. "Though I'd have to figure out how to disable it first, in case a child found it. Would a glob of superglue in the moving parts take care of that?"

Jake didn't even blink at this conversational side track. "Not permanently. It would be a mess to clean, though." He paused, a signal he was switching back to the original conversation. "But if they take you in for questioning, I'll make sure your lawyer brings up that you're not the only one with access to the garage."

"I'm not throwing you under the bus," Penelope protested.

"Think of it more as sowing confusion among your enemies," Jake suggested.

Put like that, Penelope could see the logic. Knowing that her husband understood her well enough to know how to blatantly manipulate her relaxed something in her chest. "You know, if they arrest both of us, Brian will have to take care of Timmy tonight," she said, the image of Brian facing an angry Timmy making her smile despite the seriousness of the situation. "Though... If they're going to bring in everyone who had access to the garage in the past few days, that includes Brian, too."

"And that might be what keeps you in your own bed tonight," Jake said, nodding toward the heated conversation between the detective and the chief. "If they just take you, with no other evidence, it could look like retaliation for letting your dog ruin some very expensive Italian leather shoes. And the department doesn't need another lawsuit."

"*My* dog?" Penelope leaned forward again. "It was *your* retirement party in *your* house." But Jake was right. If he wasn't worried about a lawsuit, Purcell could probably detain Penelope, but if he tried to hold Jake and Brian as well, he'd face a revolt.

"*Our* house," Jake corrected.

Jake had been the popular acting chief of police before Purcell had been hired, and Brian had been a senior detective. When it had become clear that Jake couldn't work under Purcell and he'd chosen retirement, half the force might have transferred to other agencies if Jake hadn't made it clear he wanted them to stay on. Even so, most of the police still called him "Chief", which irritated Purcell when he was within earshot.

Penelope glanced around. "Speaking of your dog..."

"Brian took him for a walk. As entertaining as it would have been to let him help with the search, Purcell has a gun and a serious grudge."

"Probably best," Penelope agreed.

The conversation by the front door concluded with

Purcell stomping down the driveway to his car, not looking at Penelope or Jake when he passed them. Brianna Sanchez followed more slowly, stopping near the couple. "Ms. Standing," she said with a nod to Penelope.

"Hello, Detective Sanchez."

The three waited until Chief Purcell had driven away before facing each other.

Despite her resolve to keep her mouth shut, it only took ten seconds of silence for Penelope to crack. "I had nothing to do with that gun."

"Of course not." Brianna seemed to struggle to maintain a straight face. "If you had, you never would have stored it in the garage."

"Thank you!" Penelope said, shooting Jake a vindicated look.

"And Jake and Brian would have secured it better," Brianna added.

Somehow, that felt unfair. Penelope was about to launch into her newly formed plan to disable the gun with super glue when she thought better of it.

Brianna waited just a moment longer, as if she expected Penelope to comment, and then looked at Jake. "How hard would it be for someone to get in there?"

"Well..." Jake slowly pivoted to look at the garage. "We've gotten into the habit of leaving the door open during the day when we're home."

"The neighborhood's pretty safe," Penelope said. "And the expensive tools are in locked cabinets anyhow."

"And," Jake added, "it keeps the smell from seeping into the house."

Seemingly relieved that someone had brought it up, Brianna said quickly, "What *is* that stuff, anyway? I thought it might be soap, but it looks like there's rat droppings mixed in? Is it some sort of homemade pest control?"

Jake sucked in his cheeks and stared at the cloudless sky. Penelope smiled. "It *is* soap. I'm just bad at following directions. Do you want some?"

Brianna's eyes widened in alarm. "No, thanks." Then, as if realizing her reaction might be offensive, added quickly, "I can't accept gifts from anyone involved in a case. Ethically."

Beside Penelope, Jake turned away with a fit of coughing.

"Maybe I should give Chief Purcell a case of it for Christmas," Penelope mused.

"Please wait until we get this case closed," Brianna pleaded. "There's only so much I can do."

"Fine." Penelope took a breath and set her shoulders. "So what now?"

"Now," Brianna said, pulling out her notebook, "you tell me exactly which hornet's nest you poked that's led to someone framing you for murder."

NINETEEN

Sitting at the kitchen table with Detective Sanchez, Penelope recounted all the people she'd visited connected to Brad Squires since the body was identified.

"Well, Esther, of course, but I think we can all agree that Esther isn't trying to frame us for murder. Also, she could probably figure out a way to get the gun into the rafters, but I think she'd choose a place she could get to more easily."

Brianna nodded. "I think we can strike Esther from the list."

"Okay. Then I dropped by Brad's brother's body shop. He seems to be the only person in town who didn't get ripped off by his brother. But I don't think it could be Nick who's setting up me and Esther unless he recognized me after I left." She paused, trying to decide how much she should tell Brianna about her history with Nick Squires. "Let's just say that we didn't part on good terms the last time we interacted, so I got out of there before he remembered who I was."

With a sigh, Brianna kept writing. She had tiny precise handwriting, and Penelope thought she could probably read it, but she would need to squint, which would be too obvious.

"And then I met up with Brad's ex-wife, Rosella. But I don't think she would frame us because she seemed really worried about it being pinned on Esther because of the restraining order. I don't think she was acting, either."

Brianna flipped a page and kept writing. "Anyone else?" It was clear she expected the answer to be yes.

"Well, Jake and I went to The Big Secret. You know, the dinner theater and male revue? It's kind of amazing — all the employees got together to form a collective and now they're really making it work." When Jake coughed gently where he stood waiting for the coffeemaker to finish, Penelope reined in her tangent. "Anyway, Vincent Collins works as a bartender there. And playwright, too. You know he was in business with Brad?"

Brianna nodded.

Before Penelope could continue, the front door opened and Brutus barged through the kitchen, sniffing everyone in case they might have left food for him. Brian followed, more slowly. "Purcell's gone, right?"

The other three people spoke in a chorus. "Yes."

"Good. He was having just a little too much fun going through all your stuff." Brian opened the refrigerator to put the bag of treats inside. "By the way, you might want to avoid that house around the corner for a couple days. The guy came outside and yelled about dogs peeing on his lawn and Brutus nearly washed out his mailbox post while we were talking."

Brianna groaned. "I know exactly who you're talking about. He moved to town three months ago, and he's averaging three calls to the PD per day."

"Hm. Probably going to be four today," Brian said with a

shrug. "Someone ought to talk to him about waving around that bat, though. I suggested it was a bad idea and he seemed to think I was threatening him."

Penelope had been crossing the street to avoid that house, as had most of the people walking dogs in the neighborhood. She suspected the problems with his lawn were due to over-watering and a resultant grub infestation, but her one attempt to convey that had been cut short by her sense of self-preservation.

Seeing Brutus sniffing at Brianna's notebook as if wondering whether it would be good to eat, Penelope patted her leg twice to get his attention and then pointed at his bed in the corner. The dog reluctantly wandered over and threw himself down on the padded bed, as if trying to prove how much torture he endured every day, but he ate the treat Jake tossed with alacrity and was snoring twenty seconds later.

Brianna shifted in her chair. "So you talked to Vincent Collins..."

Penelope dragged her attention away from the neighbor around the corner. "Yes. Though I can't see him trying to frame us, either. He just seemed so excited to have another person coming to the show." She glanced back at Jake. "We're definitely going."

"The dinner theater," Jake clarified. "Not the male dancers."

Brianna was nothing if not persistent. "So... Brad's brother, Brad's wife, and his business partner. That it?"

"Almost. Jake and I went to the Caribou Diner for dinner and spoke to Big Wayne."

"You're talking about Wayne Fauta?"

"Yes. He was Brad's boss at the parks and recreation department, and he's the one that got fired when Brad embezzled all that money. But he seems genuinely happy being the night manager at the diner, and I'm pretty sure he's asleep during the hours we have the garage door open, so it couldn't be him."

Putting her pen down on the table, Brianna looked straight into Penelope's eyes. "Please tell me that's it."

"Yes. I mean, Jake and I also went over to Wags Forever, but that wasn't related to Brad Squires. You don't have a dog, do you?"

"I... no." The detective seemed confused by the conversational turn.

"Good. I mean, it's not good that you don't have a dog if you want a dog, but good that you aren't spending a lot of money for someone to drive your dog to the edge of town and stick them in a boring kennel all day. If you do get a dog, talk to me before you enroll them in a doggy day care. That Happy Dog Day Care place is a complete racket."

"Okay." Brianna looked back over her notes. "How did you find the time...? No. Never mind." She flipped her notebook closed. "Thank you for speaking to me."

"You're welcome," Penelope beamed. "What happens next?"

"Next, I and the rest of the detectives figure out who killed Brad Squires. And you should probably make sure you have the number of a good lawyer. My 'she would never put it in the garage' defense of you is only going to last so long with Chief Purcell. It would be really helpful if he wasn't reminded that you exist in the next few days." At this, she looked from Penelope to Jake.

Jake rubbed his face with one hand. Next to him, Brian laughed silently.

Penelope smiled. "Would you like some coffee before you go? It's better than the stuff at the station."

"No, thank you." Brianna pushed back from the table and stood up. "At the rate my week is going, I'd probably get written up for taking bribes from a suspect."

Brian guided her out of the kitchen. "Cheer up, Sanchez. Maybe you'll get something useful from the gun." Something in her silence must have given him an answer, because after a brief pause, he added, "Or... maybe not."

"We ran the serial numbers. It's registered to the victim. And I doubt we're going to get any useful forensics after twenty-five years."

Brad had been killed by his own gun. There was some sort of irony in that. Or possibly just karmic justice. Certainly it was support for studies that proved that bringing a gun into the home increased the owner's chance of being shot.

Penelope heard the front door close, and since Brian didn't immediately return, she assumed he'd gone outside with Detective Sanchez. She looked up at her husband as he placed a cup of coffee in front of her. "I have to admit, the only times I worried about leaving the garage door open, it was about people taking things, not storing guns in the rafters."

"Same here."

Penelope considered as she drank her coffee. "This seems like a onetime thing, but if you would feel better with it closed during the day, I can package up all the soap and send it to Chief Purcell."

Jake's back was to her as he poured another cup, but she could hear the smile in his voice. "You know, the feds get involved if you send threats through the mail. Better not chance it."

Penelope laughed softly into her mug. Then she thought about people going through all her things and sobered. "At least we learned something important from all this."

Sitting down across from her, Jake braced himself against the table, as if preparing for a gale to whip through the kitchen. "I'm always delighted to hear about what you consider important."

"This time it's about the case," she promised. "Somebody got worried enough to try to pin the blame on Esther and me." She stopped. "Or is it Esther and I? That's not right, is it?" She ran through the sentence in her head, removing Esther from the equation. "Esther and me," she concluded with confidence.

Patience practically seeped from Jake's pores. "Someone got worried enough to try to pin the blame on Esther and you and...?"

"Oh. Well, when we found out about all the money Brad was carrying when he disappeared, we thought the murderer could have been anyone, not just someone with a reason to hate Brad."

Jake gazed into the distance as he thought about that. "Except if he'd been killed as a crime of opportunity, there would be no reason to misdirect the investigation."

"Exactly!" Smiling, Penelope said, "Now we know Brad wasn't killed by a stranger for the money. It means we're on the right track."

TWENTY

This time, Penelope showed up at the community center ten minutes before the start of Rosella's self-defense class. Rosella was already there, moving chairs to the edge of the meeting room.

The lawyer beckoned Penelope in as she stacked another chair. "More questions, or are you here for class?" She was once again dressed in a black, knee-length, narrow skirt with low heels, but this time her blouse was a deep blue.

"Both, if you don't mind." Penelope grabbed another chair and moved it to the edge.

"Not a problem. I can stick around a few minutes afterward." She glanced down at Penelope's shorts and sneakers. "Is that what you usually wear during the day?"

"Yes. Do I need to change?" Penelope remembered the previous session and how dressed up the women had seemed. Having a dress code for a self-defense class seemed odd, but there was undoubtedly a reason.

Rosella gave her a reassuring smile. "Not at all. I prefer people to practice while wearing whatever clothes they normally wear, especially their shoes. We build muscle memory here, and different clothes and shoes can make it harder to access when you need it. I do ask that you remove any jewelry that might scratch someone or that might get caught on something."

Penelope's plain gold wedding band had been chosen specifically so she wouldn't snag it on anything or harm an overenthusiastic pet, so she left it on. But she pulled her phone out of her pocket and put it down on a chair so it wouldn't get broken.

Two women came into the room and put their purses on chairs near the door. They called hellos to Rosella and smiled in welcome at Penelope even as they moved the last few chairs. Both women had been at the previous class.

After two more women hurried through the door, Rosella glanced at her watch. "Let's go ahead and start. Today we're going to work on elbow strikes," she said as she wandered to the doorway and released the door from the stop that held it open. It swung slowly closed. "But first we're going to practice yelling."

Without warning, Rosella suddenly yelled, "Hai!" The sound was short and sharp and so unexpectedly loud coming from such a small person that Penelope jumped.

Rosella smiled encouragingly. "We — especially women — often respond to danger by staying as quiet as possible. How many of you were taught not to make a scene in public?" When she paused, every woman nodded. "An attacker is counting on that. So a powerful yell can be your most effective weapon, scaring them off because they know you're not going to stay quiet."

She placed her hand over her diaphragm. "The other thing a good yell does is focus your energy. It's harder to be scared if you yell. So we're going to practice. One, two, three. Hai!" She paused, listening. "Louder!"

Still self-conscious, Penelope's first efforts were weak. But at the end of five minutes, her shouts were as forceful as the others', and she was raring to fight.

From there, they moved to elbow strikes, both in front and pivoting to someone behind them. As the only person without a partner, Penelope practiced with Rosella, who gave her tips as they repeated the moves in slow motion. "Lift your elbow and then rotate with your hips so you get your full body behind the blow. Good."

The move wasn't difficult, but it took Penelope a while to connect the movement of her hips with the motion of her arm in such a way that her strike had any power behind it. It felt like only a few minutes had gone by when Rosella stepped back and looked at her watch again. "Great job, everyone! I'll see you next time. Bring your friends with you!"

The other four women left in a cheerful — and louder — group. Penelope stayed behind to talk to Rosella about the murder, but half her mind was still on the class. "Is it weird that I found that fun?"

Rosella smiled. "I try to get everyone's adrenaline pumping, at least a little." She sat in a chair and pulled a bottle of water from her purse. "You had more questions?"

"I don't know how much the police have told you..."

The lawyer shook her head and drank. When she was done, she recapped the bottle. "Not much, but I haven't asked."

Penelope took a moment to organize her thoughts. Then she explained. "It seems likely that Brad was killed the last night you saw him." When Rosella opened her mouth to protest, she added, "The postcards could have been written in advance and then mailed by someone else when the message was relevant."

Rosella's mouth closed as she considered that. "That's... I guess that's possible. Everything was either super specific but bound to happen at some point, like me wearing that dress, or it was vague enough that I filled in the blanks, like my son's costume." She snorted and shook her head. "That man was a snake."

As much as it pained her, Penelope left that snake slander unchallenged. This information was too important to risk derailing the conversation. "We know your ex-husband wrote the postcards, so he must have planned to have someone else mail them, but I haven't talked to anyone that knew of any friends of his."

"That's because he didn't really have any by that point." Rosella stowed the water bottle in her purse. "Brad had three good friends from high school, but by the time he left, two were dead and the third was in the army, stationed in Germany. I think he joined up partly to get away from Brad."

Penelope noted the third man's name just to be thorough, but if Rosella was right about his reasons for enlisting, she doubted she would have been involved, even if he'd been in the country at the time.

"At one point I thought Vincent Collins was a friend," Rosella continued, "but they weren't even speaking to each other by that point. Brad's brother... Nick was tired of cleaning up after him. I don't think he would have done that."

That matched with everything else Penelope had heard about Brad — belligerent, prone to seeing everyone else as a mark, and in general a person with very few redeeming qualities. But *someone* had been mailing those postcards after his death and there was one possibility they hadn't explored.

"I hate to bring this up," she said, "but is it possible he had a girlfriend?"

Rosella folded her hands together in front of her. "At the time, I would have sworn up and down that he'd been faithful." She stopped and shook her head, as if marveling at her past self or maybe the entire situation.

"But now?" Penelope prompted when the silence lengthened.

The other woman nodded once, a decisive gesture. "Now I have a lot more experience with how abusive partners act and how most accusations are really confessions. Brad regularly accused me of flirting with other men. He checked the mileage on our car to make sure I wasn't going anywhere he didn't know about. Grocery store runs were timed." She blew out a long breath. "You get the idea."

"I'm sorry." The words felt inadequate, but there was nothing else Penelope could say.

"Thank you." Rosella took out her water bottle again, though she didn't drink. "To answer your question, I think it's pretty likely he had a girlfriend, or maybe more than one, on the side. But I don't know who any of them were, so that's not all that helpful."

"Do you think," Penelope asked, choosing her words carefully, "that your son might have an idea?"

Without moving from her seat, Rosella pulled away from Penelope.

Chances were, Rosella's son, Tim, wouldn't want to dig up memories of that time, but Penelope was running out of people who might have known, and parents forgot their children soaked up everything around them.

Penelope leaned forward. "I wouldn't ask if it wasn't important. Someone is trying to frame Esther for this, and she's the last person who deserves to be accused." Trying to imagine how she would react if someone suggested talking to Seth about a childhood trauma, Penelope added, "You could ask him yourself, or I could talk to him if he's willing. Obviously, I don't want to dig up the past if that would hurt him, but Brad *was* his father, and he deserves to know what happened to him."

For two long seconds, the women sat in silence.

Finally, Rosella nodded. "I'll call him tonight and see if he's willing to talk to you. No promises. Let me get your phone number."

After they'd exchanged contact details, the two women left the room, and the mood lightened. "If I don't get arrested in the next few days, I'm coming to your class," Penelope said. "Who knew yelling would give me so much extra energy?"

Rosella smiled. "It's even better when my co-instructor puts on the padded suit and you can practice the moves at full speed without worrying about hurting anyone. He's in Bucharest for a family wedding, but he should be back in a few weeks."

That *did* sound like even more fun. "I'll have to leave space in my schedule."

They had reached the doors that led from the building to the parking lot when Rosella stopped, one hand on the lever. "You should ask Vincent Collins about the girlfriends. Not that he knew at the time," she hastened to add. "But if Brad had a girlfriend, I would bet he gave her a deal on a fireplace insert. Vincent might still have paperwork you could go through."

And then Rosella pushed open the door and strode out into the parking lot, petite and confident — a powerful phoenix risen from the ashes of her former life.

TWENTY-ONE

The next morning, Penelope unexpectedly found herself near The Big Secret. Her planned walk with Ranger, a ten-month-old chocolate lab, had taken a detour when she'd seen a loose horse in the middle of the street with three police cars blocking traffic. Penelope could have told the officers chasing after the nervous horse that they'd have more luck with a calmer approach, but she doubted they would listen to her. In any case, the last thing the horse needed was an excited dog barking, so Penelope turned the corner a few blocks early. "We'll take the long route to the park," she promised Ranger.

For his part, Ranger was delighted to have a new array of plants and fence boards to sniff and leave his mark on, but Penelope urged him to keep moving past the small business district so they could finish their walk before midnight.

A box van advertising gin was parked in front of The Big Secret, and Vincent Collins was holding the door open for a young man in shorts and a polo shirt, pulling a hand truck loaded with boxes. Considering how much of the dinner theater audience had been too young to buy alcohol,

Penelope was surprised the bar went through that many bottles of hard liquor. Then she remembered the audience at the one and only male revue she'd attended. "The problem wasn't the men dancing," she told Ranger. "It was the women around me who felt they had to scream constantly to get their money's worth. I think they were trying to convince each other they were having fun."

If she'd known about the yelling during self-defense classes, she would have staged a quiet revolution and taken the group there. As it was, she'd pleaded a headache and slipped out before anyone noticed. It hadn't even been a lie. That had been back in the days when she'd been trying to find friends by fitting in. Looking back, she could have saved herself a lot of effort. After all, it wasn't as if she hid her personality well enough to fool anyone.

Keeping a close eye on Ranger so he didn't pee on anything important — such as a person or the carpet just visible through the open doorway — Penelope waved to Vincent and approached. "Hello again!"

"Hello! You're a little early..." He trailed off and stared at the street behind her. Penelope turned and saw the bay mare trotting down the center of the street, steel-shod hooves ringing on the asphalt, tail and head held high. The delivery driver let his hand truck settle as he watched the sight. Three police cars followed the horse, red and blue lights reflecting from every surface.

Vincent shook his head. "Are they *trying* to scare that poor horse with all those lights?"

"Oughta make a barricade in front of it," the delivery driver said, leaning on the handles of the hand truck now.

Ranger whined, fully prepared to race the horse or, more likely, get kicked in the head. He wasn't a stupid dog, but he was still young and convinced of his own omnipotence. Penelope tightened her grip on the leash and offered him another treat for sitting nicely.

Suddenly, a young girl, maybe ten years old, whipped out from a side street on an electric scooter and zipped up next to the horse. In one swift move, she tossed a sweatshirt, caught both sleeves under the mare's neck, and abandoned the scooter to put her free hand on the bridge of the nose while she ran alongside. Hanging with most of her weight on the horse's neck, her feet only touched the ground every ten feet.

"Ah, crud," said the delivery driver, abandoning his wares to sprint toward the horse. But his steps slowed as mare and girl came to a stop before the next intersection, both of them breathing hard.

Then the girl looped her sweatshirt sleeves around the horse's nose in a crude halter, easily turned her in a circle, and walked her onto a nearby lawn.

Vincent clapped, and the delivery driver joined in. Before Penelope had finished giving Ranger another treat for lying down, a pickup truck pulling a horse trailer pulled up next to the girl and horse, blocking the view.

"Where did the *horse* come from?" Vincent asked, but he didn't seem to expect a reply.

The delivery guy shrugged and muscled the hand truck through the door. "I used to deliver fresh produce to a zoo, and even with all the weird stuff I saw there, this town still takes the cake." There was a clink of bottles as he set the boxes down and came back for the next load. "Nice dog."

"He is, isn't he?" Penelope was always happy to share her pride in her charges. "His name is Ranger." Then she finally remembered the reason she had stopped by. "Vincent, I talked to Brad's ex-wife, Rosella, last night." As she spoke, she remembered Rosella was technically Brad's widow, not his ex-wife. He'd been dead when the divorce decree had been finalized, even if nobody had known it. "She thinks Brad might have had a girlfriend. Or maybe more than one."

Vincent waited for the delivery driver to pass through the door with another three boxes. "Would I be surprised? No. He didn't take any of his promises seriously. But I don't know who they were. We didn't exactly sit around and drink beer together. By the time I bought his half of the business, it was a struggle to keep things civil long enough to get the papers signed."

Penelope nodded. "But Rosella had a good idea about that. You know all those installations Brad did without telling you? You eventually figured out who they all were, right?"

"It was either that or have their deaths on my conscience," he said glumly. "I bought full-page ads in the paper for a month begging people to contact me, *and* the reporters wrote a front-page story about it."

Front page news in a larger city might have been a big deal, but the front page of the local paper often had beginning piano recital reviews and in-depth reports on the reorganization of the shelves in the grocery store. Warning people of a potential fire hazard in their home actually *was* news, but Penelope suspected there would have been complaints that it had bumped something important to the second page.

"Do you still have those names? Rosella thought Brad would have likely cut his girlfriend a deal."

"Huh. I might. Let me think for a minute." And think he did, staring up at the sky. Across the street, the horse trailer pulled away, the mare visible through the slats. The girl who had caught the horse shoved something in her back jeans pocket, tossed her sweatshirt over her shoulder, and walked down the street to retrieve her electric scooter, which a police officer had picked up.

Closer by, the lift gate at the back of the delivery truck whirred to life, rising until it was level with the interior. Penelope squinted, trying to see how the controls worked. If Ranger hadn't been there, she would have walked over to look, but the dog's posture told her he was a little unsettled by the strange noise, so she fed him more treats and praised his bravery in staying there when such a big scary machine was running.

Penelope was so intent on reinforcing the good behavior that she'd nearly forgotten about Vincent when he spoke.

"Email. It'll be somewhere in my email since I had to send a list to the company who sold us the things and to my lawyer when I was going through bankruptcy." He wrinkled his nose. "Might take me a while to find it, though. I have thirty years of messages in that account and I've never been good about organizing it. But I'll look for you. I sometimes have downtime during the show."

Penelope gave him her contact details again. Afterward, he looked at Ranger. "Would you be willing to have your dog on stage? I need a dog actor for our next play."

Penelope tried to imagine Ranger following cues on stage while there was food and a bunch of people who might pet him just a few feet away. Anything was possible, and he'd certainly do better than Brutus, but the chance of the dog wandering off was pretty high. On the other hand, the dog ignoring all stage directions and running around in the audience might be the draw that the new play needed.

"Ranger isn't mine, but I'll ask his people if they'd be willing to make him a star."

"Thank you." Vincent took the clipboard from the driver and signed it without looking.

Deciding that she'd tempted fate long enough with Ranger's bladder, Penelope encouraged the dog to stand. "You'll let me know if you find the list? Thank you."

And they made it past the delivery truck to a light post before Ranger stopped to make his mark.

TWENTY-TWO

An unexpected job chasing a cat around on the owner's roof and then fixing the screen that had caused the problem in the first place threw off Penelope's schedule such that she didn't have time to check her email until she and Jake were ensconced on the couch after dinner. "For a geriatric cat with three legs and only one eye, Lonny is pretty spry," she admitted, snuggling into her usual spot with her back against Jake's shoulder and her legs stretched out along the cushions. "We did three laps around the eaves before I could catch up."

Jake flipped from one channel of golf to another. "I take it luring him with treats didn't work?"

"It might have, if Michelle hadn't used an entire bag before she called." Over his long life, Lonny had perfected the art of grabbing treats and dashing away before he could be grabbed. "He was pretty full."

"I think I would have just waited until he came back inside."

"That's because you don't know Lonny." Penelope shifted her legs to the side so Brutus could get on the couch without stepping on her. "In his prime, Lonny was a legend in the neighborhood. There was no trouble he couldn't get into. He would have qualified for a bulk discount at the vet if that was a thing." Lonny's former owners refused to keep him inside and then moved to another state, leaving their cat behind. If Michelle hadn't adopted him and restricted him to the indoors and attached cat patio, Lonny wouldn't have made it to his current ripe old age. "How was your afternoon?"

"Brian and I looked at three houses and I had two potential client meetings."

"Any of the houses look good?" She would have asked Brian, but he'd gone out for drinks with former coworkers. Penelope suspected it would be an evening of grumbles about Chief Purcell.

"Water damage in the first, termites in the second, but the third looked like it might work. The guy who owns it did a few weird modifications, but nothing that should affect the structural integrity. We're going to take another look at it tomorrow. Maybe talk to the neighbors."

That was a promising sign. Brian had only reached the "talking to the neighbors" stage once before. Five minutes of interacting with the couple next door made it clear why three houses on that block were for sale.

"And the clients?"

"One got scared off when I refused to guarantee results. The other signed the contract and left a deposit. She wants me to track down some missing jewelry without involving the police so we can confirm who took it. I doubt it's going to take long."

Penelope considered that as she waited for her laptop to finish updating. "So she knows who stole it, but doesn't want to get them in trouble."

"She has three nephews and one has a record, but she's convinced he's changed his ways." Jake switched back to the previous golf channel and set the remote down. "I'll look into that tomorrow. We have the appointment at..." He paused, searching his memory. "Cherish Pets? All those names sound sort of the same."

"Nurture Pets," Penelope corrected. It was one of the two alternates to Wags Forever that Jake had agreed to vet for Esther.

"Right. Nurture Pets." He paused as the golfer lined up the ball and swung, then sighed in disappointment at the resulting slice. "The appointment's at two. If you're not in jail by then."

Penelope knew she shouldn't laugh, because it really wasn't funny, but she still snorted. "Promise you'll bake me a cake with a file in it?"

"Are you kidding? I fully expect you to talk your way out of the cell in fifteen minutes or less. Well before Timmy is due for insulin, anyhow."

Amid the sales offers, spam, and client queries, two unfamiliar senders in her email inbox caught Penelope's attention. "Vincent Collins found the list of people Brad had secretly installed fireplace inserts for." When she clicked on the attachment, she blew out a sharp breath. "Twelve people, all women. I think that might answer the question of whether he had a mistress."

"Twelve?" Jake muted the television and turned his head to look at her screen. "Who has that much time? Didn't he have a small child at home?"

Penelope reached back to pat his shoulder. "Always so practical. Hopefully, most of these women were just regular customers. But we'll have to track them all down." A few of the names looked vaguely familiar, like maybe she'd met them at PTA meetings when her son was younger.

"Forward them to me. I'll have Brian start on that list in the morning."

Penelope tapped the button and sent Jake the attachment. "It's kind of nice, you having someone to dump stuff on."

"Work with," he corrected.

"Sure. We'll call it that." She opened the next email. "Oh!"

"Something good?"

"Rosella talked to her son and he got back to me." She scanned the email, then read it aloud. "'As you can imagine, I have mixed emotions about my biological father's death. I'm not convinced that finding and punishing his killer will bring any additional closure to those affected by my father's actions. However, my mom tells me that someone is trying to blame Miss Esther. She was a bright spot in a horrible year, and if this will help her, I'll answer any questions you need to ask.'"

Penelope paused. "I hope he has someone near him that he can talk to. Doctors are famous for bottling everything up, and that's not healthy."

Jake hummed in agreement. "Did he remember anything that might help?"

"He..." Penelope read through the rest of the message. "He spent a few afternoons around a woman he thinks was named Jenny or Josie, who had long red hair in a braid. Brad told him he wasn't allowed to mention her to his mom, so Tim thinks there was something going on."

She switched back to the list Vincent had sent. "Two Jennifers, a Joanna, and three Jessicas. People really aren't very imaginative when they name their children."

"Says someone named Penelope."

"That's my point. My parents went out of their way to make sure I was the only one with my name in my class. It could have been worse. If I'd been a boy, my name would have been Winfield." She paused to let that sink in. "But seriously, if everybody had a little more originality, things would be different. Those keychains they used to sell with names on them would have had a greater variety, for one." A disappointment in childhood had been her inability to find her name on any pre-printed items, no matter how hard she searched.

"Do you want me to get you a keychain with your name on it?"

"Now it's all done to order, so there's no point. You can get one that says *anything*." Brutus grunted, as if to give weight to her words.

"Ah. So you only wanted one because you couldn't have it."

Penelope took a breath to protest this calumny, then stopped. "Maybe. But it was still unfair that all seven Jennifers in my grade could get a mug with their name on it and I had to use a permanent marker."

"Your villain origin story, in fact."

Put like that, it sounded less like a child's complaint and more like the trajectory that made her who she was. "If I'd been the eighth Jennifer in my class, I might have grown up to be a completely different person."

Jake leaned over to kiss her temple. "I kind of like the person you turned into."

"That's handy because I kind of like the person you turned into, too." Penelope closed her laptop and set it on the coffee table. "How long do you think Brian will be out?"

"At least another two hours. Did you have something in mind?"

Penelope smiled and twisted to look at him. "We *could* clean and reline the kitchen cabinets like we've been meaning to do for the last two months."

Jake moved from her temple to her nape. "That sounds like something the eighth Jennifer would want to do," he murmured against her skin.

"I don't know. The eighth Jennifer is probably a villain origin story all in itself. But maybe we should leave the cabinets for another time and go to bed."

Brutus sighed loudly, making them both laugh. Penelope extricated her feet from beneath the dog. "I'll get something to keep Brutus occupied and meet you upstairs."

TWENTY-THREE

When Penelope came home for lunch the next day, she found Brian taking up most of the kitchen table, laptop open in front of him along with a legal pad filled with his neat angular printing plus a mug, napkin, and a plate with evidence of breakfast. He glanced up when she entered. "Hang on, Pen. Let me get this cleaned up."

"No rush. I haven't decided what I want to eat yet." Her phone dinged as yet another client wanted to set up an appointment. It had been doing that all morning, making Penelope worry that the software had been blocked and she was getting requests from the last two months, but she'd deal with that when she sat down to work them into her schedule.

Jake's low voice and the jingle of distant tags told her that her husband was in his office with Brutus. Penelope opened the refrigerator and stared at the contents. "How did it go last night?"

"Good. Saw a lot of people and we had a good time. I won a few games of darts and lost some money on pool." He stacked his dishes and brought them to the sink. "Everyone promised to be extra nice to you if you get arrested."

"That's good, I guess." Picking up a container of macaroni and cheese, she lifted one corner and sniffed, then put it on the counter along with the broccoli and leftover pierogies. "Jake said you saw a house you liked yesterday?"

"Yeah. It backs up to the park on East Street. I went over this morning to get a feel for the neighborhood and I wasn't getting any red flags."

Penelope let the refrigerator door close. "I have a couple clients over there and I've never had any problems, for whatever that's worth. You're not bothered by those twelve-foot skeletons, are you? Almost everyone on that street has them out for Halloween."

"I'd be willing to buy one of my own to fit in." He closed his laptop and put the pad of paper on top. "Jake had me run those names of women who'd had Brad Squires install their fireplace things off the books."

"Anything interesting?" Penelope scooped macaroni and cheese and broccoli on her plate, mixed them together, and added pierogies on the side before popping the plate in the microwave. Then she turned around to give Brian her full attention.

"One is ninety, which would have made her sixty-five at the time, so I think we can rule her out."

"Probably." Back when she'd been in her twenties, sixty-five had seemed ancient. Now that she was in her fifties, it seemed middle-aged. "That brings it down to eleven."

"Two have since died, and one moved to Scotland. We can't count them out, but I'll move them to the bottom of the list since it's going to be harder to get information."

Penelope refrained from commenting on the fact that

Brian seemed to equate moving to Scotland with dying. "Leaving eight women who are still alive and in the area?"

"Yes. And there's one familiar name, though I can't see how it's anything but coincidence. Jessica Green."

Because she'd separated the investigations so completely in her brain, it took Penelope a moment to place the name. "Jessica Green, from Wags Forever?"

"That's the one."

After pulling her food from the microwave, Penelope ignored the stack of pot holders within easy reach and shifted the plate from hand to hand until she could drop it on the table. She slid into a seat, then got back up and returned with a fork. "I looked at that list last night. How did I miss her?"

"Because back then, she was Jessica Harper. She married Victor Green two years after Brad Squires disappeared. She and Victor divorced three years later, but she kept her married name." He shrugged. "I can't find anything linking her to Brad, though. Coincidences happen, especially in a town this size."

Thinking of Wags Forever, Penelope said slowly, "Pugahoula."

"Excuse me?"

"There might be a link between Jessica Green and *Nick* Squires. Is that relevant?" She told him of the dog Nick had described and seeing a very similar dog during their tour of Wags Forever. "But the link might just be that Nick and his wife use Happy Dog Day Care and some of those dogs were borrowed to make it look like Wags Forever had more dogs staying there."

Brian wrote a note next to a name. "That's pretty thin."

"Yeah." Penelope pushed her plate to the center of the table and stood. "Guard my lunch."

At the doorway to Jake's office, Penelope waited as Jake finished his phone call. Brutus ambled over to have his ears scratched and then walked past her. She heard him lap water from his dish in the kitchen.

"Thanks for your time," Jake said, and pulled his head-phones off. Noticing Penelope for the first time, he smiled slowly. Even after years together, that expression made her heart beat faster. "If you're here, it must be time to take a break. Calling pawnbrokers," he added, explaining why a break was needed.

"Did you ever get a chance to talk to Nick Squires about his dog?"

"I did, though we had to get through all the car talk first." He frowned. "He's got some odd ideas about where to source parts for older models. I'm not sure I would trust him to work on my vehicle."

As much as she wanted to hear about the dog, Penelope couldn't help herself. "The man is a menace! I don't under-stand how his business is still open."

"Because there aren't enough good mechanics, so even the bad ones find work." Jake held up a finger before she could respond. "But getting back to your question... He said the dog goes to work with his wife every day. And *she*..." He paused, building up the moment. "*She* works as a dog walker for Happy Dog Day Care."

Jake sat back in his chair and put his hands out.

Penelope considered that. "So we can draw a line from Jessica to Nick's wife to Nick to Brad." She blew out a breath. "That's not very direct."

"No, but it still means we should move Jessica to the top of that list of women."

"I agree." Penelope raised one eyebrow. "You know, most

women wouldn't be happy to find out their husband had a list of women. But I wouldn't change a thing."

"Not even my socks?"

"Okay, maybe that." Jake's insistence on keeping socks with holes in them did bother Penelope. "But other than that..."

Out in the kitchen, Brian gave a wordless oath. "Come on, buddy. You promised to stop doing that." He raised his voice. "Sorry, Pen!"

Penelope had a very good idea of what Brutus had done to provoke him. She gazed at Jake. "And maybe your dog, who I think just ate my lunch."

Jake stood up and grabbed his phone and jacket. "Let me make it up to you. We'll go out to lunch on the way to Nurture Pets."

TWENTY-FOUR

Nurture Pets looked more like what Penelope expected from a pet rescue. The office was in a strip mall next to a dry cleaner, Chinese restaurant, and a gas station. The front two-thirds of the space was a second-hand goods store, with everything from cat trees to clothes, and the back was a jumble of unsorted items with a computer desk shoved into the corner under the outstretched arms of an eight-foot-tall Godzilla. Yacht rock played softly over the speakers, and the whole place smelled vaguely of wet dog.

Penelope felt at home.

A woman in her twenties sat behind the cash register with a chemistry book open in front of her and a knitted scarf draped around her shoulders. She looked up and smiled brightly when Penelope and Jake came inside. "Let me know if you need help finding anything." Then her scarf moved and Penelope realized it was an elderly cat wearing a sweater.

Jake said, "We're here to meet with Cathleen Dreiser."

The woman twisted in her chair to look at the back of

the store, then turned back to them. "All the way in the back. You can't miss her. Don't worry about DeeDee."

"Thank you!" Penelope grabbed Jake's hand and pulled him with her. This was the sort of quest she loved, one that suggested there might be trouble if they looked hard enough.

"Who or what do you suppose DeeDee is?" Jake murmured as they walked past a coat rack filled with feather boas.

"I don't know, but I'm not worried about her." Penelope halted to look at a bright red rain jacket with yellow ducks on it. "Remind me to try this on when we're done."

DeeDee turned out to be an ancient toothless chihuahua whose tongue hung out the side of her mouth. She was sleeping in a basket next to Cathleen, who was, as suggested, impossible to miss since she was the only person in the back section. She was in her sixties, had her bangs dyed purple and the rest of her chin-length hair dyed blue. Penelope wondered how much effort it would take to maintain those colors. Jake sighed softly next to her.

Cathleen stood up and shook their hands. "Hello, have a seat! Wait, let me find you something..." A scuffle with the nearby furniture ensued, and Penelope ended up perched on a rocking horse while Jake slumped on a barstool under the arms of Godzilla.

When Cathleen returned to her regular office chair and pulled out a manilla folder stuffed with information sheets, Penelope briefly wondered if the seating arrangement was an odd power play, but she decided in the end that Cathleen had merely found them something that she would be willing to sit on. It was a compliment, in a way. Penelope leaned to the right and the horse slowly rocked.

Cathleen handed them each one sheet, obviously a copy

of a copy, nearly to the point of illegibility. "I think every-thing is on here. What questions did you have for me?"

Penelope abandoned Penny Wheeler and her backstory and went with the truth. "We have a friend who's looking into end-of-life planning and we wanted to check out what's available. How does it work with the animals in your care? Do you have a shelter or...?"

"We get them into permanent foster homes as soon as possible," Cathleen said. "Nurture Pets guarantees care for the rest of the pet's life. Food and medical bills are paid for by the trust. But the idea is to get them into another home situation, not warehouse them until they finally die of old age."

"What if nobody wants to take them on?" She tried to remember how Esther had described the dogs. "I think she called them four horrible rat terriers that bite everyone who walks through the door."

Cathleen laughed, the sound swallowed by the clutter. "You'd be surprised how many of our dogs come in with that description. If Grandma's dogs were easy to handle, the relatives would take them and she wouldn't have to come to us."

That made sense. Penelope had found new homes for a few animals after their owners had passed away, but they had all been relatively well-behaved. Brutus was the only one who had ended up staying.

Cathleen continued. "But honestly, if they bite everyone who walks through the door, why aren't they closed up in another room when strangers come over? It's all about managing the environment and setting the animals up for success." She scanned the info sheet and pointed to the third column. "We have a trainer and a behaviorist that we work with."

Jake shifted on the stool and knocked Godzilla's fingers, then threw an arm around the figure to keep it from rocking backward. "The trust is funded through donations when the dogs are accepted?"

Watching her husband talk financial strategy while hugging a towering Godzilla was almost too much for Penelope, and she had to look away for a moment to keep from giggling. Near her feet, DeeDee began to snore, tongue flapping on every exhale.

When Cathleen had finished explaining that everything was funded through donations and the thrift shop, Penelope glanced up again. Jake had abandoned the stool in favor of standing. He checked with her to see if she had more questions, and when she shook her head, helped her off the rocking horse. "Thanks for your time."

"Of course, of course." Cathleen stood to usher them to the front of the shop. "And there's information on the sheet about becoming a permanent foster, if you're interested. I have the feeling you two would be good with difficult dogs."

Penelope felt a swell of pride that they could be so easily identified as good dog parents, and resolved to talk to Jake about fostering later.

Once they were on the sidewalk, Jake laughed under his breath. "Quick, make sure we didn't agree to donate our kidneys while we were in there. That woman is dangerous."

"We *are* good with dogs," Penelope protested.

"We had to go to a restaurant because our dog ate your lunch."

"Okay, sure, Brutus isn't perfect, but the pizza delivery people haven't boycotted our place like they did with his previous owners."

"It was a very near thing," Jake reminded her.

"Close only counts in horseshoes and hand grenades. Brutus is much better behaved than he used to be."

Jake laughed again. "There's still a lot of room for improvement. What did you think of Nurture Pets?"

"I thought I was going to have to practice my elbow strike on Godzilla back there." Penelope got into the passenger seat. "But I had a much better feeling about this place than I did about Wags Forever. And *not* just because she said we were good with problem dogs."

"I agree. I'll look at their filings, but I think this is an option for Esther's friend." He paused. "Is it just me, or has your phone been going crazy all afternoon?"

Penelope dug her phone out of her pocket, a feat which involved some contortion since she didn't want to unlatch her seatbelt. "I've been getting tons of notifications of pet sitting requests all day, but I haven't had the time to sit down and deal with them."

Thanks to Jake and her son, Seth, Penelope's business was no longer run from a paper calendar, a bunch of scribbled notes, and forgotten invoices. Now she had a website and scheduling software, which was helpful if she needed to have Jake take over some of her appointments.

She could never shake the feeling that gremlins in the machines would mess it all up, leaving her with no idea of what she had promised to do and leaving animals unfed. Seth swore the system was reliably backed up, but Penelope still wrote each appointment in a notebook when she made it. If the computers ever took over the world and locked her out of the software, she would still have a way to reconstruct her schedule.

Jake glanced at her phone, which had buzzed again. "Could be bots trying to break in to the site. I'll have a look when we get home."

But when they arrived at the house and Penelope sat down at the kitchen table with her laptop, she found a series of genuine requests, all for walking dogs in the middle of the day. Her worry that the system had somehow been hoarding messages for the last few weeks also turned out to be unfounded; Jake looked into the log files and assured her these were all new.

"Somebody must have decided to get out of the business," she said as she replied to messages and tried to work out how she would add a dozen dogs to her schedule. The answer was: she couldn't, not unless she started walking dogs together. But some of them were outside the area she covered, and if Jake helped, it was just on the edge of possible.

Her husband tapped on his own laptop. "I have an idea about that." A few seconds later, he turned his computer around so she could read the screen. It showed a tiny article from the website of the local paper, published just before noon.

Penelope read aloud. "The popular dog sitting service Happy Dog Day Care abruptly closed their business this morning, leaving multiple clients waiting in vain for the distinctive 'Happy Dog Bus' to pick up their pooches. The business, which advertised its kennel-less day care service, charged a premium to take a carefully selected group of dogs on multi-hour hikes through open spaces. One client, Valerie Dumas..." Penelope stopped and looked at her own screen. "Yep, she's on the list. A shih tzu named Parfait."

Jake cleared his throat. "Can a shih tzu really roam the wilds for six hours every day? That probably should have been a clue that they weren't doing what they said."

"Right?" Penelope shook her head and found her place again. "Blah blah blah Valerie Dumas, whose dog, Parfait, has been picked up every morning for two months, said she received no advance notice. When Parfait hadn't been picked up by ten o'clock, she reached a recorded message saying the day care had been permanently closed. Happy Dog Day Care has not responded to a request for comment. This story will be updated for the weekend edition."

She swiveled his computer back in his direction. "This can't be just because they saw the quadcopter, can it?"

"I wouldn't think so." He was quiet for a moment as he watched her send messages. "Tomorrow's going to be taken up onboarding new clients. What do you think about visiting Jessica Green this evening? We can try to catch her at home."

"You have her address?" Then Penelope shook her head before he could answer. "Of course you do." Even if Jessica Green was no longer at the house she'd been at twenty-five years ago — and it was possible she *was* since it hadn't burned down because of the fireplace insert; Penelope had checked — property records were public.

"It would mean we won't be able to go to Steel-toed Magnolias tonight, though," Jake added. He sighed theatrically.

Penelope kept a straight face as she met his eyes across the table. "You know you're only delaying the inevitable."

He smiled. "Yes. But we never know what the future will bring. I live in hope."

TWENTY-FIVE

Jessica Green lived in a nearly new condominium on the north side of town. From the sign on the corner, one of the units had recently sold, but that sign was almost always there. The condo board didn't allow more than one For Sale sign on the corner at a time, to keep it from looking like the owners were all trying to flee, so normal turnover meant that the sign had achieved a semi-permanent place in the pristine white gravel.

Penelope hadn't been inside these condominiums because the condo association rules didn't allow any pets. She looked at the buildings, all identical in everything from the paint color to the single sago palm in white gravel at the corner of the building.

"It's just as well they don't allow pets here," she said, gesturing at the spiky green leaves. "Those things are super toxic to dogs." Unlike onions, garlic, and the milk chocolate found in American candy bars — all relatively benign foods that pet owners obsessed over — the seeds of a sago palm would kill a dog.

"I'll be careful not to plant one in our yard." Jake took

her arm to guide her through the gap between two units to the one beyond. "Building nine should be back here."

But that structure turned out to be building four, which was odd because it was nowhere near its adjacent numbers.

"Who numbered these things?" Penelope asked when the next unit had the number eight.

They followed the path to the next building, which was five. "Maybe this is what happened to all those people who memorized two hundred digits of pi in high school," Jake offered.

Penelope wasn't sure she'd ever heard of pi until her son had needed help with his math homework in eighth grade, but she let that go. "If you started a rescue to take care of pets after their owners die or can't keep them anymore, would you live in a condo complex that didn't allow any pets?"

"You mean even if we didn't have Brutus?"

"Obviously." Building eleven gave way to building seven, and given the identical nature of all the units, Penelope couldn't remember how to get back to where they'd started. Luckily, Jake had an excellent sense of direction. "Also assuming I wasn't around, since I'd never live here."

"Ah. So if I was a totally different person." He made a show of considering that as they rounded another corner. "No. Too much beige. But I see your point. It's a little weird. Aha!" That last comment was in response to seeing building nine nestled between two and fourteen.

A worn doormat that said "Welcome" in a stylized font was the only thing that differentiated Jessica Green's unit from all the others. "I wonder how often people get home and try to walk in the wrong unit," Penelope said as she rang the doorbell.

"Probably depends on how much they drink," Jake said before the door was yanked open and Jessica looked out.

Gone was the friendly and professional woman from Wags Forever. This version had wild hair falling from a ponytail on top of her head, pink velour sweatpants, and a long orange t-shirt that proclaimed that someone had gone on a vacation to Florida and only brought her back that stupid shirt. She had a half-full glass of wine in one hand. "You two. I should have known. I suppose you're here to talk about Happy Dog?"

Speaking of drinking... Penelope was fairly certain that wasn't her first glass. Jessica seemed to be waiting for an answer to the question, so Penelope gave her a tentative "No?"

In his most soothing voice, Jake said, "We wanted to talk to you about Brad Squires."

Jessica blinked. "Brad Squires. I should have known he would show up again someday." She glanced at the slim watch on her wrist. "I have twenty minutes to kill. Tell you what — I'll answer your questions if you answer mine." She turned and walked away, leaving the door open behind her. "We're well beyond the statute of limitations for any crimes he and I committed. Come on in."

Penelope didn't hesitate. Jake might have qualms about questioning someone whose judgment was impaired, but he was used to defending his case in court. Penelope didn't care if everything Jessica said was inadmissible as long as she talked. If Detective Sanchez needed to build a case later, she'd find some other way to get the information.

To the right of the door was a dining area with a glass-topped table that would seat six, though it was crammed in an area in such a way that two of those people would have difficulty getting into their seats. A wooden bowl of fake fruit sat squarely in the middle, next to a pile of mail. Jessica grabbed two more wineglasses from where they hung in the pass-through to the kitchen and sat down at the head of the table, waving them to sit down. "Good old Brad."

Penelope took the chair nearest Jessica, leaving Jake to sit on her other side, which coincidentally left him close to the stack of mail. She took the glass Jessica had poured and swirled the wine, trying to look as if she knew what she was doing. Wines had never been a passion of hers, but she could see from the price tag on the bottle that it was the type that encouraged people to sniff and say it tasted of things like hay and apricots. "So you knew him."

"Oh yes, I knew Brad." Jessica poured another glass and handed it to Jake. "Then again, I think Brad knew a *lot* of women." She leaned back in her chair and looked at them. Penelope thought Jessica might be more sober than she'd implied when she'd opened the door. Possibly that was her first glass. "Is it true he was dug up from under a rosebush?"

Penelope nodded. With four people there when the body was found, plus all the police and everyone else involved with the case, that had to be common knowledge.

Jessica shook her head slowly, as if in wonder. "It *had* to be his wife, though I never would have imagined she would have the guts to kill him." Then she shook her head more decisively, this time rejecting what she'd said. "No, it has to be a coincidence. His wife wouldn't say boo to a goose."

Feeling like she'd missed a chunk of the conversation, Penelope returned to the point where things had stopped making sense. "What does him being buried under a rose-bush have to do with anything?" Next to her, she could feel Jake flipping through the mail on the table, his actions hidden by the bowl holding the fake fruit.

"I'm allergic. Break out in hives when I get near the

things." Jessica toyed with the stem of her glass. "Even ended up in the emergency room once when they served mint tea that had rose hips in it at my sister's baby shower." She sipped her wine. "It's ridiculous. Roses are supposed to be the most hypoallergenic flower out there, and it's the only thing I'm allergic to." Waving a hand at the window behind her, she added, "It's why I moved in here. Nobody can plant anything that isn't approved by the board, and I'm on the board. At least I *was*. With this place in escrow, I really don't care anymore."

Penelope scrunched up her nose. "But sago palms? Really?"

Jessica's brows drew together in confusion. Under the table, Jake tapped Penelope's foot. She sighed and went back to asking questions about the more important topic.

"So you and Brad were a..." She almost said *couple*, but did that really apply when the man was married and living with his wife? "You were together."

Jessica had noticed Penelope's search for the right word. "Please don't tell me you're here to moralize about my affair with a married man."

Penelope shook her head. "The only one breaking promises was Brad." It was true that if she and Jessica had been friends at the time, Penelope would have distanced herself, but she'd never understood society's insistence that the "other woman" was always in the wrong when it was the man who had stood up in front of everyone and promised to be faithful. "But you *were* together when Brad was installing those fireplace inserts. How long did it last?"

Jessica looked up at the ceiling, remembering. "From November until he left me standing in my house with my bags packed." She took a larger drink from her wine. "For the last twenty-five years, I thought he was on a beach somewhere in Latin America, laughing at how stupid I was to help him set up his escape."

This was the first person Penelope had spoken to who had admitted knowing Brad was planning to leave that night. Had Brad really intended to take Jessica with him and been killed before he left? Or had Jessica found out her lover was abandoning her and used his own gun to shoot him? But something about the postcards had been bothering her, and this might explain it. "You told him what to write on those postcards."

Raising her glass in a toast toward Penelope, Jessica gave a small, triumphant smile. "The postcards were my idea. You don't disappear with a bunch of the city's money without somebody looking for you, but a six-month head start would have let us cover our tracks. We had it all worked out — a flight to Costa Rica and new names and passports. Then we'd buy a boat and live on that while we sailed along the coast until we picked out the perfect spot to run a dive charter business. It would have been glorious."

Glorious for Brad, perhaps. Penelope suspected Jessica would have found the hidden side of the man soon enough. Then, isolated from friends and family, in another country, and with no money of her own, she would have been lucky to survive.

Penelope knew there were far more men in the world like Jake than Brad, but the Brads of the world destroyed everything they touched. The town had probably been a safer place for more than a few people after Brad was planted beneath that rosebush.

"So you helped Brad write those postcards." They knew Jessica hadn't written them for him, because the handwriting was Brad's and his fingerprints were on them.

"Of course I did. Brad reacted to things, but he wasn't

very good at anticipating events. If it had been up to him, he would have just sent birthday and anniversary postcards. Except he didn't know the dates. And that wouldn't have convinced anyone. No, he needed me to tell him that teachers went back to school a few weeks early to get their classrooms ready, and the kids had a costume parade before Halloween."

Penelope took a slug of wine to hide her distaste for Jessica's pride. Brad had taken that knowledge and written postcards meant to terrorize his victims — and it had worked. "But if you were planning on flying to Costa Rica with Brad, who was going to mail them at the right time? You couldn't just have someone mail out specific cards at specific dates. That person had to make judgment calls."

"Yes, that was another woman Brad *knew*. His sister-in-law, in fact."

Given Brad's relationship with Rosella, Penelope assumed the relation was on Brad's side of the family. "Nick's wife? Or did he have other siblings?"

"Nick's wife, Jenny. I met her once."

Penelope raised an eyebrow and leaned forward just a bit, all the while wondering if there were any women around her own age that weren't named some variation of Jennifer.

Jessica took the bait.

"We went out to a bar one night, me, Brad, Nick, and Jenny. Nick and Jenny laughed about how she'd been dating Brad — this was before Brad was married — when she and Nick met, and then she ran off with Nick to Vegas and got married. Their son was born that year. My guess? She found out she was pregnant and picked the brother who seemed more stable. But Nick had to know, so if it didn't bother him..." She shrugged. "It's just as well. Jenny died about a year after Brad disappeared — a car crash. If she'd married Brad, their kid would have been an orphan."

"Probably let her husband work on her car," Penelope grumbled bitterly.

Jessica laughed, an honest laugh full of humor. "That's cold. I think I like you. But no, it was a drunk driver who crossed over into her lane and hit her head-on."

So Nick's wife, Jenny, had been the one sending the postcards for the six months after Brad disappeared. Had she known he was dead? Or had she assumed Brad had gone off to Costa Rica as planned, ditching Jessica along the way? They might never know.

And yet... If Jenny had been dead for over twenty years, who had planted the gun in Penelope and Jake's garage?

Jessica set her glass down and crossed her arms on the table. "My turn to ask questions. How did you figure out the rescue was a scam?"

TWENTY-SIX

Penelope froze, hoping her expression didn't show her thoughts. She'd known Happy Dog Day Care had shut down, and they'd suspected there was a link from that business to Wags Forever, but the way Jessica was acting, it sounded as if Wags Forever had also closed. Nothing Jake and Penelope had done would have scared her into closing up shop. Something else must have happened, but Penelope had no idea what.

Luckily, Jake had finished his perusal of the mail and took over. "What attracted our attention in the first place? Or what convinced us it wasn't legit?"

"Both."

"As to what attracted attention in the first place... you'd have to ask my client. She hired me to look into Wags Forever."

"Okay, fine. Where did I screw up in the tour?"

Penelope might have hesitated to answer that question, since Jessica clearly wanted to know so she could do better with the next scam. But Jake answered easily enough.

"The Pugahoula."

Jessica narrowed her eyes. "You *have* to be kidding."

"It's not even a breed," Penelope objected.

"There just aren't that many of them around," Jake said. "Nick Squires talked about the one his wife owned, and then we saw a nearly identical dog that was supposedly in the long-term care of Wags Forever. It was a little thing, but it stuck out. Everything is easier to pick out after you find the first lie."

"Huh." Jessica reached out to grab the wine bottle and refill her glass, no longer pretending this was a social occasion. "I can't wait to tell Nick that this was all his fault. He saw Penny, here, talking to the veterinarian and immediately blamed me, saying I must have let something slip, but it was actually him and Trina and their stupid dog who couldn't possibly stay in the same kennels with all the other dogs."

Penelope ran through her mental list of people involved in the case and came up blank. "Trina?"

"Nick's wife. His new wife. We've been friends since grade school." She looked from Penelope to Jake. "This whole thing was all Nick's idea. He pulled money out of his shop and used it to lease some land outside the city limits. Trina would run a dog boarding kennel and I would offer to take in dogs if owners added a bequest in the will."

"But they had to donate a certain amount *now* to reserve a spot," Jake suggested.

Jessica tilted her head toward him with a smile. "That was supposed to be the real moneymaker. When we set it up, we planned to shut it all down in less than a year."

It was a tidy little con. If they chose their victims carefully, there was little danger of dogs actually needing a place to live.

"But you didn't shut it down in a year," Jake said.

"No, because Nick got a great deal on the lease and the idiot signed for five years. He said it would look even more legitimate if we added a building for the rescue. You'd be surprised how many people don't bother to look at anything other than the glossy brochure. But some people want to see the place, and word gets around if you can't show anything. Plus, then we could start boarding cats as well as dogs."

She laughed. "And then six months ago Trina saw one of those viral videos with dogs getting on the dog bus to go off to day care. Nobody would pay premium rates to have their dogs sit in a rusty old horse stall, but she built this fantasy that the dogs would be out hiking all day long. And people bought it." She paused as she imagined it. "If we had started with that, we could have made bank with minimal risk. She's not even breaking many laws." She shook her head. "But that's not where we started. So we had all this baggage."

Penelope considered that. "And if you waited too long, people who had reserved space for their pets started dying or moving into long-term care homes and you had to take their pets." That would have been the time to move from a dodgy rescue to a legitimate business.

Jake supplied the missing piece. "Let me guess. You'd over-sold the number of spaces available."

"I'd planned to close the place before it was ever an issue," Jessica protested. "Then suddenly I had all these dogs to care for and the food bills alone were killing our profits, not to mention the vet bills."

Penelope kept her hands in her lap so she wouldn't be tempted to throttle the woman. "Where did all those dogs go?"

"Relax," Jessica said, taking another sip from her wineglass. "Nothing bad happened to them. We re-registered their microchips to invalid phone numbers and dropped them off at the shelter during the night. They would have adopted them out, so they ended up with homes in the end."

Penelope considered how that would work out for four horrible rat terriers that bit everyone who walked through the door. If they were really as bad as advertised, the county shelter would have considered them a liability and might have refused to adopt them out. Jessica was blithely assuming that all dogs that went into the shelter were adopted, but that wasn't always the case. As the woman at Nurture Pets had put it, *If Grandma's dogs were easy to handle, the relatives would take them and she wouldn't have to come to us.*

Jake was more aware of legalities. "You say that Nick had the original idea, but it's your name on the paperwork and you were the one who signed the rescue's taxes."

"Ah." Jessica leaned back in her chair. "You've put your finger on my problem. Everything between us was done with cash, so there's nothing leading back to Nick, and — at most — Trina could get a fine for keeping dogs in kennels that don't meet the county's standards. But me... I could be looking at actual jail time."

And yet, somehow Jessica didn't look as worried as Penelope would feel if she'd defrauded people and had finally been caught.

Maybe Jessica was just one of those people who didn't worry about things that hadn't happened yet. Or maybe she thought a good lawyer could solve the problem.

When her phone buzzed, Jessica glanced at it. "That's all we have time for. My ride is here." She threw back the rest of her glass and stood. "I don't suppose you could help carry my luggage, could you? The drivers can never find the right unit, so I'll have to meet the car at the curb."

Or possibly, Jessica wasn't planning to stick around to face charges.

Jake stood, and Penelope noted that he deliberately angled his body in a way that left Jessica a clear path to the door. "Leaving town?"

Jessica smiled. "One thing I learned from Brad is how important it is to cut and run when it's time."

Frowning, Penelope stood and said, "I'm not sure Brad learned that lesson himself, or he wouldn't have ended up in an unmarked grave." Then she remembered all the problems with the grave markers. "Well, he still might have ended up in an unmarked grave if he'd died from something else, but there would have been a funeral first."

A brief wave of confusion washed over Jessica's face. Then her expression cleared. "In a few hours, I'll be on a beach drinking a margarita and I will raise a toast to Brad and then never think of him again."

Penelope thought that was more than Brad deserved. Though maybe it was possible he would have become a better person if he'd lived long enough. She'd certainly met people who had changed their lives for the better. Of course, she'd also met people who had continued to damage everyone around them until they died in their beds at a ripe old age. That was the trouble with not being omniscient — she couldn't wish destruction on her enemies without worrying they might have chosen a better path later.

"Feel free to stay as long as you like," Jessica said as she extended the handle on a rolling suitcase that had been sitting behind the living room sofa. "Just pull the door closed behind you. My realtor has the key."

Penelope couldn't believe Jessica was going to get away. She glanced over at her husband, expecting him to step forward and do something, but he was standing in what Penelope thought of as his politely waiting stance.

True, he was no longer in law enforcement, but this seemed like a time for a citizen's arrest... though Penelope had only the vaguest idea of when a citizen's arrest was valid and what sort of crimes it covered. Depending on how one looked at it, there was a thin line between a citizen's arrest and just plain false imprisonment.

There was a knock on the door.

Jessica shook her head as she rolled her suitcase across the carpet. "Just my luck. The day I find a driver who can actually find my unit number is the day I leave town for good." She pulled the door open.

Detective Sanchez stood on the doorstep with two uniformed officers behind her.

TWENTY-SEVEN

"It was amazing," Penelope told Esther the next day as she sat down at her friend's kitchen table to tell her the news. "You should have seen the look on her face. Probably mine, too, since I didn't know Jake had texted Brianna and I was upset Jessica was getting away. Brianna filed fraud charges this morning. Now Jessica will have to wear one of those ankle trackers if she gets bail, because there's no way she can argue she isn't a flight risk when she had plans to leave the country."

Penelope had talked to four new potential clients already that morning, and felt she deserved some time to relax with a friend who didn't expect her to respond to every question like a normal adult. The best part of being a pet sitter — aside from being her own boss, which was a necessity with her temperament — was that dogs and cats didn't give her funny looks when she said random things.

"I wish I'd been there." Esther sprinkled flour from a measuring cup into the bowl balanced on the scale in front of her. She was putting together pre-measured scone kits for the Rose Garden Society auction, one of the group's biggest fundraisers. Esther's scone mix was an auction favorite.

Penelope had never measured ingredients by weight before, but she'd also long ago accepted that baking wasn't a skill she possessed. Improvisation in baked goods only worked when the baker understood what they were doing. Until then, it was a matter of following instructions, not one of Penelope's strengths.

Esther paused, watching the number on the scale, and then sprinkled a little more before setting down the flour. "What's going to happen to the animals that were in her care?"

"There weren't any dogs — she'd already dumped them all at the shelter. Most of the cats we saw were boarding while their owners were gone. The rest are being transferred to other rescues. It's good that you noticed the red flags. Who knows how long she would have kept defrauding people?" Penelope looked at the plastic containers full of already-measured scone mixture in front of her. "What am I supposed to be doing here?"

"Tape the instructions on the side."

Feeling a bit as if she'd been given a task meant for a small child who demanded to help, Penelope arranged the tape and the stack of printed cards in front of her. The baking instructions were simple — add a cup and a half of heavy cream, cut the dough into triangles, and bake. Maybe she *could* bake something like this. Penelope reflexively checked around her before she tore off a strip of tape. "Where are the cats?"

"Frito was being a pest when I got out the flour, so they're locked in their room until I'm done measuring."

"Smart move." If *Brutus* had been present, half the ingredients would have been in his mouth the first time anyone got distracted. Penelope taped the card to the first container, then pulled it off and rotated it so the instructions weren't upside down. Silhouettes of Victorian women holding tea cups and leaning toward each other had been printed around the card, making it look like hot gossip was flying around a meeting. "I wonder what they're talking about."

Esther glanced up briefly to get context, then went back to measuring salt. "Probably the water feature Belinda Clark put in the front yard."

Belinda and Charles Clark didn't have pets, but Penelope had delivered mail to the address often enough to know which house Esther meant. In the previous week, the lily pond had sported a new knee-high sculpture, a nod to Cellini's *Perseus with the Head of Medusa*, though in this case it was Medusa holding a man's head. Having just recently taken an online class on influential Italian artists as part of her self-improvement plan, Penelope had been so proud of catching the allusion that she hadn't considered whether people would be offended. "It's a little different, but is it really *that* weird?"

"Take another look the next time you go by." Esther sealed the container and added it to the pile before putting an empty container on the scale. "The head has Charles's features."

"Ah." Having a gory sculpture based on mythology was one thing; bringing real people into it was another. "I take it their marriage counseling hit a snag."

"He slept with her sister."

Penelope winced. "That would do it." Some betrayals would be harder to get beyond than others.

"But *apparently* he claims they're even because she slept with his father, though you didn't hear that from me."

Letting the hand holding the tape dispenser drop to the table, Penelope stared at her friend, trying to imagine why anyone would remain in a relationship with all that going on. "Talk about awkward family get-togethers..."

Esther snorted. "Can you imagine?"

Penelope could indeed imagine it, mostly because Jake had an inexhaustible supply of stories featuring family celebrations that required police intervention. The idea of the extended Clark family reunion reminded Penelope of what Jessica had said about Nick Squires's first wife. "Did you ever meet Jenny Squires?"

Esther's hands stilled as she thought. "Jenny Squires. Ah, yes, Tyler's mother." The flour bag rustled as she scooped. "Tyler would have been a few years above your Seth. Jenny was hard to read. Some of the other teachers thought she was a little slow, but I think she was just one of those people too busy observing to interact much." Esther picked up the salt. "What does she have to do with the Clarks?"

"Nothing, as far as I know. But Jessica said Jenny had been Brad's girlfriend before she'd married Nick. According to her, Tyler was probably Brad's child."

Esther raised her brows. "If so, Jenny did her child a huge favor by marrying Nick. I know you're not a fan of the way Nick runs his business, and it sounds like he's involved in that rescue mess, but Tyler was a happy kid. And Nick certainly seemed involved in Tyler's life, so he either didn't know or didn't care."

Not caring would be fine. Ideal, even. But not *knowing* sounded dangerous, as that sort of secret could come out at any time.

In any case, Esther's evaluation of Jenny Squires tallied with the postcard sender's need to know everything that went on in town. Penelope relayed that as well. "Sounds like Jessica might have been right about who sent out the post-cards after Brad was dead."

"Another mystery solved."

"Yes, but Purcell's only interested in one thing." Penelope tore off another strip of tape. "You would think he would be grateful. If it wasn't for me, nobody would even know Brad Squires was dead. Now we know *where* he was buried, *when* he died, *how* he died, and we have at least ten motives for *why* someone would kill him."

"Somehow," Esther said dryly, "I don't think gratitude is the main emotion Chief Purcell feels toward you."

"Probably not." Penelope looked at the container of scone ingredients in her hand and wondered how much Esther would be bothered by the card being a little crooked. She could take it off and try again, but that would probably just leave it more wrinkled and crooked in a different way. Shrugging, Penelope decided it was legible and that was what really counted. Besides, Esther knew how Penelope did things — if she'd wanted it to be perfect, she never would have assigned the job to Penelope.

Having dealt with that issue, Penelope went back to thinking about the murder. "Brad packed, left his wife and son, presumably with the money he'd embezzled from his day job, met up with Vincent Collins and signed over his half of the fireplace business for another stack of cash."

"According to Vincent Collins," Esther added.

"Good point. We know Brad didn't get on the plane with Jessica, so what else was he planning to do before leaving?" Penelope used her fingernail to smooth a wrinkle in the tape.

"That's only *if* Jessica told the truth," Esther said. "You only have her word that Brad was taking her with him. Or maybe he was, but they had an argument and she shot him."

They both considered that for a moment, the silence only broken by cat paws running against a closed door. Frito didn't like being excluded from the action for long.

Penelope picked up the next container. "Even if we ignore that Jessica's allergic to roses and definitely would have chosen a different spot to bury him, I'm pretty sure she would have left the country if she'd had that money."

Esther looked at the salt container in her hand and then at the dry ingredients in front of her and then back at the salt. With a slight shake of her head, she added more salt.

Penelope thought of another question, but before she could ask, her phone buzzed with a message from Jake. *Purcell came by. Thinks you sent a glitter bomb to his house.*

She picked up the phone and called him. "It wasn't me. I swear."

Her husband's voice was faintly amused. "I told him it would have required a credit card purchase, and I'd have seen it if you had." He paused. "He thought that meant I would have stopped you, and I decided it might be better to let him keep believing that."

Penelope took a deep breath and let it slowly out. "That's a tough one. Rub his nose in how sexist he's being or stay out of jail?"

"I realize that's a serious dilemma for you," Jake said. "Call me selfish, but I'd rather you stayed out of jail."

"Hmph." Letting Purcell think everything she did had to be pre-approved by Jake galled her, but at least she knew *Jake* didn't think that. She decided she would be the bigger person and let Purcell think whatever he wanted — at least until the next time they met. With that, she switched topics. "Whatever happened to the car?"

"The car?" Suddenly, Jake's voice had real concern in it. "What about our car?"

"No, not our car. What happened to Brad's car? Did it ever show up anywhere?" According to Rosella, Brad's car had disappeared at the same time Brad had, one reason everyone thought he had left town with the money. But if he'd never left, the car should have been somewhere. That might give them a clue about where he went after leaving Vincent Collins.

"I don't know. I *could* ask around." There was a long pause, which Penelope recognized as a sign that Jake was trying to decide on the best way to word something she wasn't going to like. "It might be better to leave this to Brianna. She's a good detective."

"She is, but how long before Purcell decides she was the one who sent him the glitter bomb? Or worse, asks her to waste her time tracking down the sender?" Penelope doubted Chief Purcell would ask any of his male detectives to work on something so obviously outside their scope of duties, but she suspected he was one of those leaders who thought nothing of asking the women who worked for him to take care of extra tasks that sucked up time and brought no credit.

Besides, Penelope gave even odds that the entire station had been involved in sending the glitter bomb. If so, not much work would be happening as they all dealt with an enraged Chief of Police.

Jake sighed. "I'll ask. But do me a favor and try to avoid irritating Purcell if you see him today."

Penelope crossed her fingers. "No glitter jokes, I promise."

"Now repeat that without having your fingers crossed."

Jake knew her too well. Penelope sighed, loud enough

for him to hear her through the phone. "Fine. I promise I won't make any glitter jokes if I see him."

"Thank you. I'll let you know if I learn anything."

Penelope put her phone down and looked at Esther. "Jake's going to check. I have to get going, but I'll let you know if I learn anything interesting."

"Keep the glitter jokes to yourself," Esther reminded her.

Penelope smiled. "You're no fun at all."

TWENTY-EIGHT

Amuse and Ebenezer Bruges — better known as Moo and Neez — snuffled in the grass next to the fence, inhaling the story of those who had recently gone by. Collectively, the two chihuahuas weighed less than Brutus's tail, but they were convinced they could terrorize any large dog they came across.

It was Penelope's job to keep them away from any canine that might take up the challenge, which would have been easier if their owner hadn't insisted that they visit the dog park daily. Penelope had been known to place them on the ground in the dog park just long enough to snap a quick picture to send to their owner before scooping them up and taking them on a long walk elsewhere, but mostly she just avoided the busiest times of day. Today there was only one other dog nearby, a German shepherd named Cletus on the other side of the fence in the large dog section, and he was standing on the concrete walkway at the other end, too far away for the belligerent little pair to notice.

Cletus's owner, a woman in her forties that Penelope thought *might* be named Nicole or possibly Amy, leaned against the fence between the two areas. "Did you hear about the whole dog bus thing?"

Penelope nodded. "Was your dog...?"

"Part of that group?" Nicole-Amy laughed, and across the park, her dog raised his head to look at her before returning to his sniffing. "I don't have that kind of money. Besides, Cletus doesn't like the great outdoors. He doesn't even like standing on the grass here." She lowered her voice, though they were the only two people in sight. "My cousin lives next door to the woman who drove the bus, and *she* said they've been doing all kinds of upgrades to the house lately, but all the contractors were turned away yesterday. Everything stopped, just like that."

"Hope they weren't in the middle of anything important," Penelope said, idly wondering if the cousin had been there twenty-five years ago. "But doesn't the husband own a body shop or something? I thought that kind of business always made money."

"Not with the kind of reviews he gets. When I got rear-ended, his shop wasn't on the list my insurance company sent me."

Penelope felt mildly gratified by this proof that she wasn't the only one who had been unhappy with the results of Nick's work. But he'd stayed in business, so somebody still patronized that shop. If she'd had the money back when her son had been a customer, maybe she'd have sent Nick Squires a glitter bomb. Though she wasn't sure glitter bombs had existed back then. And maybe glitter wasn't such a big deal if you already spent the day covered in motor oil.

She reminded herself not to mention glitter if she ran into Chief Purcell.

Before Penelope could come up with any more questions to ask, Cletus wandered toward his owner, and Moo and Neez charged the fence, growling and barking as if they were rabid wolves instead of tiny dogs whose legs would snap if they jumped off anything taller than three feet.

"Sorry," Penelope mouthed over the din, but she wasn't surprised when Nicole-Amy clipped on Cletus's leash and headed to the exit. The chihuahuas threw themselves at the fence a while longer and then snorted and wandered away.

Penelope's phone vibrated. Another text from Jake. *Brad's mint condition cherry red 1972 Mustang hasn't been registered since the year he disappeared. No mention in any database.*

Presumably that bit about the database meant nobody had been caught joyriding in the stolen car and it hadn't been towed from an airport lot after being abandoned.

Back when everyone thought Brad had died months after he'd last been seen in town, working out what had happened to his car seemed like a waste of time. It could have been anywhere, and finding it wouldn't have brought them any closer to the truth. But now they knew Brad had never left. So whoever killed him would have had to dispose of the car.

Penelope thought about how she would make a car disappear. Probably roll it into a pond or river. It seemed like missing person cases from seventy years prior were constantly being solved when someone found a car submerged somewhere, and any hiding place that lasted seven decades would be enough to ensure whatever secrets it held would be gone.

Maybe the car had been stolen from wherever Brad had left it and it had never shown up again because it had been taken apart at a chop shop. Though... she had a vague feeling that classic Mustangs weren't generally the cars most chop shops handled. Not that she'd ever seen a chop shop. Jake would know. She'd ask him when she got home.

Penelope had never paid attention to car prices, but she suspected a classic Mustang in good condition would have been worth something, even twenty-five years ago. So why hadn't Brad's killer forged the registration and sold the car? That would have been the easiest way to get rid of it. It wasn't as if Brad was going to report it stolen.

Two Siberian huskies, Cloud and Buck, came into the dog park as Cletus left. Penelope waved to their owner — Justin, maybe? — and corralled her charges before they could start barking again. "Come on, you two. Let's go home." The huskies were friendly dogs, but Penelope suspected they could make it over the fence separating the two areas if they really wanted to. Moo and Neez might just give them a reason.

As she left the dog park with the two chihuahuas prancing beside her, Penelope thought of one really good reason the killer might not have sold the Mustang.

It could have been the crime scene.

TWENTY-NINE

One of the best parts of owning her own business was that Penelope could set up her schedule however she wanted to. If that meant she could exercise a dog and help Esther deliver the scone packages to the auction coordinator at the same time, so much the better.

In truth, Esther was doing all the work on the delivery, with a large box on her lap as she guided her wheelchair along the sidewalks at speed. Penelope was just going along in case there were any physical barriers at Georgiana's house that would make it impossible for Esther's wheelchair to make it to the front porch.

Waldorf, a large brown dog with long legs and a bushy tail whose owner described his breed as 'Heinz 57', was content to follow along.

Penelope spent the first part of their journey telling Esther about the missing car. "I've been thinking about it, and it's not all that easy to get rid of a car. The VIN is stamped all over the place, isn't it? Even if you took off the license plates and lit it on fire, they could still figure out who it belonged to."

"Did they stamp the VIN in multiple places in the seventies?"

That required them to stop while Penelope searched on her phone. "Okay. According to this random person on the internet, it would be stamped on the engine block, the transmission, and the shock tower. Or maybe the fender aprons." Penelope looked up. "What's a fender apron?"

"Your guess is as good as mine." Esther began moving again before Penelope could look it up, so Penelope shoved her phone in her pocket and followed Waldorf, who had figured out that Esther was in charge. Esther called back, "Your point is taken, though. It would be hard to truly get rid of a car in an untraceable manner."

"How would *you* do it?"

Esther's answer was prompt. "I'd sell it to a shady Mustang mechanic and let them use it for parts."

Penelope looked at her friend with respect. "You know a shady Mustang mechanic?"

"I know everyone," Esther said. She went down a driveway into the street to avoid a small child riding straight at them on a tricycle. "How about you?"

"I'd drive it into a lake, but I like your idea. Better for the environment and you'd get some money. Though it does leave a trail back to you."

"True."

"Anyway, I doubt the car was dumped in a lake, because if the murderer did that, why bother to bury the body separately? That would be a lot of extra work, and then they'd have to worry about *two* places being uncovered over the years."

They arrived at the auction coordinator's house, and sure enough, the path leading to the front porch was partially blocked by three bags of potting soil and a giant terracotta pot. Penelope traded Waldorf's leash for the box of scone mixes, edged past the pot, and walked to the porch. The doorbell had a sign saying "Do not disturb," so she left the box and returned to retrieve Waldorf. Esther was already texting Georgiana to let her know the scone mixes had been delivered.

Penelope waited until her friend put the phone away. "The easiest way to quietly get rid of a car would be to take it to pieces at a body shop. If Nick was involved, he wouldn't have had to try very hard."

Instead of turning to go back the way they'd come, Esther motored along the sidewalk in the same direction. Penelope jogged to catch up, Waldorf excited about this change of pace. "There's not going to be anything left after twenty-five years."

"You never know what people leave lying around."

"It's not there. The bays were open when I went by and there's no place to hide a car."

"Forget about the car." Esther scowled. "I'd like to give him a piece of my mind. From what you told me, the police may never connect him to Wags Forever, but that doesn't mean he should be off the hook."

Penelope was torn between wanting to see Esther confront Nick and concern that if things escalated and Purcell arrived, *Penelope* would be the one going to jail. "Fine. Fair warning, though — if Purcell shows up, I'm leaving you there."

"Understood."

But when they turned the corner and went down the street, the auto body shop looked closed. The metal bay doors were rolled down, the open sign was dark, and the parking lot was empty.

Penelope shrugged. "Oh well. You'll have to talk to him

some other time." Preferably after Chief Purcell had forgotten about the glitter, though Penelope knew from experience that it was *hard* to forget about glitter.

But Esther was rolling across the parking lot and around the cinderblock building to look at the narrow strip of asphalt between the business and the chain-link fence behind it. "Aha!"

Penelope and Waldorf followed more slowly. The area behind the building terminated in a cement wall, creating a narrow dead-end alley that was used for employee parking and discarded bits that wouldn't fit in a dumpster, as well as a broom and an old vending machine. Halfway down the building, a familiar bus was parked. "If anyone needs proof that Nick was involved in the doggy day care scam, we can send them back here."

"Let me get a picture." Esther moved her wheelchair forward, trying to find an angle that would show both the bus and the business.

At least back here they weren't visible from the street, so nobody was likely to call the police. If they'd been younger, someone might have alerted the authorities about a potential break-in, but Penelope accepted that nobody would look at her and Esther and be concerned about crime. After a certain age, women became practically invisible. The neighbors might, however, call for a welfare check, which was both encouraging and irritating.

"Here. Hang onto Waldorf for a second." Penelope handed off the leash and then walked further down the alley to the front of the bus. From there, she could see both the side of the bus with its colorful cartoons of dogs cavorting in unspoiled woodlands and the auto shop building beyond. It was only when she backed into something hard that she looked at what else was in the alley.

She'd run into what was left of an old car. All four tires were missing along with the hood and the engine, and most of the panels were gone as well. Those that remained were covered in gray primer.

There wasn't enough left for Penelope to accurately identify the manufacturer, much less the model and year. It *could* have been a 1972 Mustang, but it might have just as easily been a 1985 Pontiac — Penelope's knowledge of cars started and ended with how to drive them. There was nothing odd about the remains of an old car rusting away behind an auto body shop; it might have been more suspicious if there hadn't been one there. Still... She scraped at the matte paint with her fingernail, trying to see what color was underneath the primer.

Was that red? She couldn't decide. Using the hem of her t-shirt, she cleaned the dirt from a larger section. Scratching at the paint with her house key felt vaguely blasphemous, but if anyone ever did anything with this car, they would need to sand the panel down and repaint it anyhow.

She cleaned the scratched area with her t-shirt and looked at it more closely. Cherry red paint peeked through the primer.

"I think this is it," she called back to Esther.

As tempting as it was to call Jake and let him relay a message, Penelope sighed and dialed Detective Sanchez. The call rolled over to voice mail. Penelope ignored the greeting as she worked out the best way to minimize her misdemeanor trespassing and emphasize the important information. "Hi, Brianna, it's Penelope. Just thought you ought to know there's a car behind Nick Squires's body shop that might be what's left of Brad's Mustang." Doubts assailed her. "Or, at least, it used to be red. It's kind of hard to tell what kind of car it is because there's not much —"

Barking erupted on the other side of the bus where Esther waited, and from the sound, more than one dog was involved in the ruckus. "Crud! Gotta go!" Ending the call, Penelope sprinted back to Esther.

Waldorf was in a standoff with an unleashed dog — Nick's Pugahoula, Penelope realized — and the two dogs were circling, snarling and barking at each other, though they weren't actually making contact. Penelope darted forward and grabbed the Pugahoula, lifting him up and stepping back. "Hush now," she told the dog, ready to shift her grip if he tried to bite her face, but he quieted in her arms.

Now that they weren't trying to prove how tough they were, both dogs looked faintly embarrassed. Jessica had used the Pugahoula's name when Penelope and Jake had been at Wags Forever. What had it been...? Muggles! That was it. Penelope wished her memory for people's names was as good as her recall of pet names, but at least she could always ask a person what their name was.

In her arms, Muggles wagged his tail and squirmed around to lick Penelope's face.

Esther said, "I'll take Waldorf back to the sidewalk and you..."

If Penelope put Muggles on the ground, he'd just charge after Waldorf again or run out into the street where he could get hit by a car. There was no getting around it. Penelope was going to have to find Nick — who must have been in the building after all — and hand his dog back to him. "I'll take care of Muggles."

But before Penelope could walk around the building, the door swung open beside them.

THIRTY

Nick Squires leaned out and took in the scene, his unnaturally black hair gaining a blue halo from the light behind him. He stared at Penelope. "You! I figured out who you were ten minutes after you left the other day."

He disappeared, but before the door had swung closed, he was back again, brandishing the ten-year-old security camera picture of her. "I banned you from the property *years* ago."

Esther coughed gently as she examined the photo. "That hairstyle was doing you no favors. Did you intend it to look like you put your finger in an electrical socket, or was that purely accidental?"

Penelope grimaced. "It rained that day and it dried weird."

Nick ignored their comments and frowned at Esther. "And *you*! You're that teacher that kept bothering my brother. What are you doing here?"

Sometimes, the best defense was a good offense. "Keeping your dog from running out into traffic," Penelope said. "Do you have a leash?"

"Just put him on the ground," Nick said with a scowl. "He won't go anywhere."

"If I put him down, he's going to attack Waldorf again. At least hang onto him until we're around the corner." Penelope moved forward and pressed Muggles into Nick's arms, using that motion to swipe the picture from his hand. She crumpled the paper, hoping no other evidence of that hair-era existed.

The dog wiggled happily and licked Nick's face. The man's expression softened. "You're a bad dog," he said to the Pugahoula, then turned and pushed the dog inside before closing the door and turning back to Penelope and Esther. "I could have you both arrested for..." He paused and frowned at Penelope's hip. Then his eyes darted toward the car rusting away at the end of the alley.

Still busy shoving the picture into her pocket so she could burn it later, Penelope glanced down. The hem of her shirt was smeared with primer gray. "Oh."

All the blood drained from Nick's face and his fists clenched.

Esther looked between them. "What?"

"He kept the car," Penelope said, tilting her head toward the end of the alley. "It's still there, or parts of it are, anyway." She stared at the unmoving man in front of her. "But *why*? You were the only one in the entire town who *didn't* have a reason to want Brad dead."

Nick didn't move, though his eyes darted between Penelope and the car. Penelope recognized that look of panic. For twenty-five years, he'd gotten away with the murder of his brother. Nobody had even *suspected* him.

At some point, he must have stopped worrying about what was left of the Mustang, because it was still out in the open over two decades later. Penelope sympathized with that because she'd put off many important tasks for so long that they seemed to disappear. Maybe nothing as important as getting rid of a car tying her to a murder, but it was just a matter of degrees.

And now, two people knew.

Esther moved her wheelchair closer. "Was it because of Tyler?"

Her words broke Nick's trance. "Tyler?" Then understanding dawned. "Oh, you mean did I do it because I found out Brad was Tyler's biological father? No. I knew Jenny was pregnant before we started dating."

"Then *why*?" Maybe Penelope should have been more concerned with calling Detective Sanchez and having Nick taken in, but she needed to know. The one motive she and Esther had considered — finding out his son wasn't biologically his — had just evaporated. Nobody had ever mentioned any feuds or fighting between the brothers. Then again, family relationships could be complicated, as she well knew.

"Because he borrowed a bunch of money from me to set up that stupid fireplace business. I gave him everything I had, which left me scrambling to pay suppliers. I took on *debt* because he convinced me he'd be seeing huge returns in just a few months and he'd pay me back."

Nick shook his head in disgust. "All I got was a bunch of excuses for why he didn't have the money. Someone defaulted on a payment. His kid got sick and insurance didn't cover everything. He had to hire a lawyer to file a restraining order because some crazy school teacher had threatened him." At this last, he scowled at Esther.

"I was protecting your nephew," she responded, steel in her voice.

At some point Esther and Nick might want to discuss

that, but right now Penelope was still trying to understand what had happened. "You killed him because he didn't pay you back?"

"Of course not." Scorn laced his voice. "What kind of person do you think I am?"

Penelope bit her lip to keep from replying, because Nick had been part of two different frauds operating the week before. Luckily, Nick kept speaking before Penelope lost the willpower battle.

"If he hadn't been able to pay me back, well... That was a risk I knew I was taking. But he drove over here that night with a bunch of postcards I was supposed to give Jenny because he was leaving town for a while. Didn't even get out of his car because he had a flight to catch. And when he opened his bag to get the postcards out, there were *stacks* of cash. He had enough to pay me back and still live like a king on a beach for a few years."

He shook his head. "My business was about to go under, he *had* the money he owed me, and he was still going to leave me hanging. So I grabbed his keys and told him he wasn't leaving until he paid me back."

Nick was quiet for a moment, staring into the distance as he remembered that night. Then he said softly, "It was an accident."

Penelope had a hard time imagining a scenario where shooting someone in the head was an accident, but she kept her mouth shut.

"He pulled a gun on me and told me to give his keys back. Then we were wrestling for the gun and... somehow the gun went off." Nick was looking at the ground as he spoke.

Penelope was skeptical about this "accidental" gun discharge that just happened to shoot Brad in the head. She *thought* she'd done a good job of keeping that off her face until she noticed Esther raising her eyebrows at her. Luckily, Esther drew Nick's attention by reverting to teacher mode and saying briskly, "Well, it certainly sounds like self-defense. A good lawyer will know what to do."

Nick's head shot up. "What? No, I'm not talking to the police."

Esther gave him a stern look. "Twenty-five years is more than long enough to live with that sort of guilt. It's time to get it all out in the open." She reversed her wheelchair, heading toward the street.

"No!" Nick leaped forward and grabbed Penelope with one large arm, pulling her back against his chest as he shouted to Esther. "You stay right there or... or I'll hurt her!"

Esther stopped.

Next to Penelope's ear, Nick muttered. "Wait. I need to think." He reached behind him for the doorknob. "I need to think," Nick repeated, more loudly this time. He took a shaky breath. "We're going to go into the office and everybody's going to sit down while I figure out what to do next."

Go along for now or try to escape right away? If Nick thought about it long enough, surely he would realize he had no alternative to turning himself in. What else could he do? Penelope had trouble imagining Nick killing them in cold blood.

But then again... He'd killed his own brother and covered it up for twenty-five years. She didn't believe his the-gun-went-off-by-accident claim. If she and Esther went into the auto body shop, it would be just that much harder to escape.

And if he opened the door, Muggles was sure to race out and square off with Waldorf again. Penelope took the safety of her charges very seriously.

She tried to remember what they had done in the self-defense class. Elbow strikes! In her head, she could see herself turning and slamming her elbow into his throat. Twist her hips, pivot, and strike.

She made her move.

Twist... Nick held her tightly against his chest, so Penelope's attempt to turn made them both spin, and her upper arm bounced harmlessly off his biceps.

They lurched on the pavement. "What are you doing?" He sounded confused.

Emboldened by her partial success, Penelope tried again, Rosella's words in her ear. Turn and *whip* the elbow back! This time she managed to squirm sideways, but Nick was still crushing her against his chest, which meant her arm was sticking out in front of her.

Belatedly, she remembered a second move. Rosella had said foot stomping worked best with hard-soled shoes, but she'd also said it worked even in bare feet. Penelope lifted her right foot and brought her heel down on the top of Nick's right foot.

He grunted and picked his foot off the ground. Since his other foot was somewhere behind her, Penelope returned to her first move. She rotated forward again and then whipped around to slam her elbow into his sternum. Who needed a teacher in a protective suit when you could practice on the real thing?

Nick let her go and stumbled back.

That was when Penelope remembered the other thing she'd learned in class. "Hai!" The yell might not have been loud enough to be heard by anyone on the street, but Rosella would have been proud.

Distracted by the yell, Nick didn't notice Esther rolling forward, holding a broom like a knight wielding a lance,

Waldorf trotting at her side. She rammed the tip into his solar plexus, and Nick doubled over, wheezing.

Esther let go and the broom clattered to the ground. "Run!"

Penelope needed no encouragement. She grabbed Waldorf's leash and the three of them fled, not stopping until they had reached the end of the street and they could hear the welcome sound of sirens.

THIRTY-ONE

When the police arrived to hear Esther and Penelope's claims of murder and attempted kidnapping, and then Nick's counterclaim of trespassing and assault, Chief Purcell immediately took Penelope into custody.

Detective Sanchez was placing cuffs on Nick Squires at the time and Esther promised to take care of Waldorf, so Penelope allowed herself to be handcuffed and taken to the police station, where she was placed in an interview room to wait.

While she was there, a large number of police officers found it necessary to drop in to tell her about the interview with Nick Squires and see if she wanted a drink or needed a more comfortable chair or perhaps a blanket.

Two hours, a soda, two candy bars, a deck of cards, and a glitter-flecked blanket later, Penelope looked up from her game of solitaire when the door opened. Vivica Hammer walked in, a red-faced Chief Purcell behind her.

Penelope had only seen Vivica Hammer, aka Hammerhead, from a safe distance before, but now she received the full impact of her presence. Her long dark hair had been braided in a circle coiled around her head like a crown, and she wore a pristine black suit and six-inch heels. Penelope wouldn't have been able to walk in those shoes, but Vivica moved with fluid grace — and with the added height, even tall men had to look up to meet her eyes.

"Say nothing," the lawyer commanded, looking at Penelope. Then she pivoted to Purcell. "My client was assaulted by a murder suspect nearly twice her size, yet was somehow detained and left in an interview room for hours with no offer of medical assistance."

Penelope opened her mouth to admit she hadn't been hurt, and she'd certainly have told one of her visitors if she had, but the look Vivica shot in her direction was so fierce that she closed it again.

The lawyer continued. "Meanwhile, by keeping my client here with no cause, you have prevented her from conducting her primary business, caring for animals. This is just the latest in a pattern of behavior, and I'll be talking to my client about suing for harassment after we leave. The longer *that* takes, the higher the requested damages." She stopped talking and waited.

Through clenched teeth, Purcell growled, "She's free to go."

"Excellent." The lawyer turned to Penelope. "Ms. Standing?"

After folding the sparkly blanket and putting the cards back in their box, Penelope accompanied her lawyer to the front desk, where her belongings were returned.

As they went through the front doors into the cool night air, Vivica began laughing. "That was fun! I don't get to do that very often. Esther says hello. Be sure to call me if that doesn't stop this nonsense." She flicked a bit of glitter from her sleeve with a manicured nail. "How many strippers does this town have...? Never mind. Do you need a lift?"

"No, thanks." Now that she had her phone back, Penelope wanted to find out where she was on her pet sitting schedule. But when she unlocked her phone and brought up her calendar, everything was marked as completed.

Even Timmy, the diabetic cat, whose unpredictable nature surprised Penelope on occasion.

Penelope shoved her phone back in her pocket. "Fingers crossed my husband still has both of his eyes."

THIRTY-TWO

Penelope sat next to Jake on the couch, applying antiseptic ointment to the four parallel lines across her husband's left cheek and blocking Brutus from licking it. "You were very brave."

Brian was having drinks with his realtor and possibly putting in an offer on the house Jake had looked at, and the only sound in the house was the quiet conversation of the cricket commentators on the television.

"It's fine," Jake said, taking the tube from her and capping it. "It wouldn't have even happened if I hadn't gotten cocky and tried to pet him afterward."

Penelope finished smoothing the ointment on the fourth scratch. "Oh, yeah, Harold loves attention after his shot, but Timmy wants to kill someone." She leaned back to look. "I don't think it's going to scar."

"It would be the height of irony if it did." Jake folded her hands in his and kissed them as he looked into her eyes. Penelope's heart skipped a beat. "You were off getting grabbed by a murderer and I got tagged by a *house cat*."

"Hey, don't sell yourself short." Penelope swiveled so she

was in her usual spot, feeling his warmth against her back and resting her head on his shoulder. "Timmy is a lot of rage in a tiny package."

"I've been in knife fights that were less scary." Jake picked up the bottle of wine by his feet and poured her a glass.

"I believe it." Penelope shifted her legs so Brutus could climb on the couch and rest his head on her thighs. "I should have been able to figure it out a lot earlier. There was no way Nick could have pulled money from the shop to invest elsewhere. He doesn't have any customers. But I got thrown off when the gun was planted. I thought it was because we'd gotten too close to figuring out who the murderer was."

"Which we hadn't," Jake said. He handed her the glass of wine and began pouring a second for himself.

"We still thought someone had killed him for the money," Penelope agreed. She thought about that as she sipped her wine. "Though, technically, Nick did kill him for the money. Or at least, the money played a large role in what happened. But before the gun showed up, we thought it could be *anybody*."

Jake cleared his throat. "And then we learned it was somebody motivated enough to get near that box of soap."

"Hey, that soap is going to outlive us all."

"Like nuclear waste." He set the bottle back down next to the couch and relaxed into the cushion.

Penelope laughed as she smoothed Brutus's ears. "My point is, I thought the gun being planted had something to do with the murder, when in fact, Nick was trying to derail our investigation into Wags Forever and Happy Dog Day Care. Remember what Jessica said? Nick panicked when he saw me talking to Dr. Marsh."

"Thus confusing us all," Jake said. "But I still don't see why you went looking for the car behind his shop today."

"I wasn't, really. But Esther said *she* would have disposed of Brad's car by selling it to someone who would use it for parts, and then I saw what was left of a car when I was taking a picture of the dog bus, and..." She waved her wineglass. "It sort of escalated from there. Do you know if they found anything in it?"

As usual when something big was happening, Jake's phone had been buzzing with updates all evening. "He got rid of the seats, but the ceiling lit up when they sprayed it with Luminol, and there's a bullet hole in the dash."

Penelope nodded. "Thus explaining why he didn't just give it to Esther's shady Mustang person for parts." The wine was cold and tart, and Penelope could already feel her muscles relaxing. "Maybe I should go to more of Rosella's self-defense classes. I kind of froze up when I needed to do something, and I completely forgot to yell until after I'd hit him with my elbow a bunch of times."

Jake's arm came around her chest, pulling her closer to him. "I think that's a great idea."

The wine and a feeling of safety combined with the softly accented voices speaking nonsensically on the television left Penelope in a pleasant haze for a few minutes. Then another thought bubbled up. "What's a fender apron?"

"In a car? It's a sheet of metal, sort of between the tire and the engine. How did that come up?"

"It has the VIN stamped on it in a 1972 Mustang."

"Ah." Jake turned his head to look at her with a smile. "It's kind of hot when you recite car facts."

Penelope snorted. "If I'd known it was that easy..."

"What can I say? I'm a simple man."

Penelope wiggled her legs out from under the dog and

turned to put her feet on the floor. She leaned over to whisper in Jake's ear. "We *could* go upstairs and I'll read you all the other places they stamp the VIN on a classic Mustang. If you're not too badly injured from your encounter with Timmy..."

Jake set his glass on the coffee table and stood, extending a hand to help her up. "There's only one way to find out."

"Shock tower," Penelope said in a husky voice. Then they both dissolved into laughter and, arm in arm, headed for the stairs.

THANK *you for reading Death Discovers a Bone! I hope you've enjoyed this book — if you want exclusive Penelope and Jake content, join my newsletter! When you sign up, you'll receive free bonus stories from both Tess Baytree and T.M. Baumgartner, and every month you'll get a newsletter full of foster kitten pictures, funny anecdotes, and writing updates. Sign up here: https://tmbaumgartner.com/subscribe/*

ACKNOWLEDGMENTS

Lots of people helped with this book, even if it wasn't always intentional. Not that anyone was trying to *sabotage* me (as far as I know), but my community helps me in ways that aren't always obvious.

First off, I have to thank my friend Jon. During one of our daily card games (over the phone), he mentioned trying to track down the gravesite of a distant relative. That gave me my opening scene, the hardest part of any novel.

Next, I need to thank my critique partners, who always read my manuscripts and come of with a solid list of ways to make the book stronger. They're also good at pointing out when I have a person, and dog, and a cat with names that are so similar that everyone got confused. The Brian/Brianna situation, however, was of my own making and isn't their fault.

Big thanks also go to my ARC team. Reviews are critical, especially for indie publishers — there's nothing like having zero ratings or reviews to make a reader think twice about downloading a book, no matter how enticing the description. I appreciate the boost!

And finally, thank you to my readers. Yes, that's you! If you didn't enjoy these books, there wouldn't be any point in writing them. I hope this book brought a smile to your face!

ABOUT THE AUTHOR

Tess Baytree is the pen name of mystery and speculative fiction author Theresa Baumgartner. At various times she has been a veterinarian, Unix system administrator, software developer, and after-hours book-shelver in a medical library.

Theresa currently lives in Northern California in a house with too many animals. She knits hats for garden gnomes and runs with scissors only when absolutely necessary.

Want updates about new releases? Silly dog anecdotes? Join the newsletter mailing list! Go to https://tmbaumgart ner.com/subscribe/ or point your phone's camera at the QR code above.

ALSO BY TESS BAYTREE

As Tess Baytree:

Death Walks a Dog (Penelope Standing #1)

Death Tracks the Scent (Penelope Standing #2)

Death Smells a Rose (Penelope Standing #3)

Death Trims the Tree (holiday novella)

Death Crashes a Wedding (Penelope Standing #4)

Death Paints a Picture (Penelope Standing #5)

As T.M. Baumgartner:

Shift Happens

The Chaos Job (Jackpot Drift #1)

The Chaos Connection (Jackpot Drift #2)

The Chaos Nexus (Jackpot Drift #3)

Dragon Freehold

All Gremlins Great & Small (The Portal Storms #0)

All Rocs Wise & Wonderful (The Portal Storms #1)

All Basilisks Wild & Sparking (The Portal Storms #2)

Theoretical Magic (The Floodmouth Files #1)

www.ingramcontent.com/pod-product-compliance
Lightning Source LLC
Chambersburg PA
CBHW031955060726
47497CB00016B/2181